The "No-Guys" Pact

Books in the Holly's Heart series by Beverly Lewis:

The "No-Guys" Pact

BEVERLY ♥ LEWIS

ZondervanPublishingHouse

Grand Rapids, Michigan

A Division of HarperCollinsPublishers

Requests for information should be addressed to:

ZondervanPublishingHouse
Grand Rapids, Michigan 49530

Library of Congress Cataloging-in-Publication Data

Lewis, Beverly, 1949– .
    The "no-guys" pact / Beverly Lewis.
       p. cm — (Holly's heart : #9)
    Summary: While trying to earn money to help a friend attend
church camp, fourteen-year-old Holly and several other girls have
fights with the boys in their lives, causing all kinds of trouble
during the week at camp.
    ISBN 0-310-20193-4 (pbk.)
    [1. Moneymaking projects—Fiction. 2. Camps—Fiction.
3. Christian life—Fiction.] I. Title. II. Series: Lewis, Beverly,
1949– Holly's Heart ; bk. 9.
PZ7.L58464Nr   1995
[Fic]—dc20
                                   95-32667
                                       CIP
                                       AC

Edited by Lori J. Walburg
Printed in the United States of America

95 96 97 98 99 00 01 02 /❖ DH / 10 9 8 7 6 5 4 3 2 1

For one of my fans,
Lisa Lease . . .
she knows why!

❤ Author's Note ❤

I've enjoyed every minute spent writing this new Holly's Heart book. The fan mail you've written, pleading for more Holly books, has been so encouraging. Thank you!

And so, my dear fans, Holly-Heart lives on.

Special thanks goes to my husband, Dave, who assisted with the manuscript, as well as Barbara Birch. My kid consultants were full of great ideas as usual. They are Amy, Julie, Shanna, Janie, Mindie, Jennifer, Jon, and Beth.

Well, by now you probably know I have a fab-u-lous editor named Lori Walburg. She too deserves lots of credit for the success of this series!

O N E

"I can't believe it. Are you sure?"

Andie Martinez nodded. Her dark eyes looked all too serious as we corralled her three-year-old twin brothers toward their backyard jungle gym set. "Amy-Liz said it herself. She's definitely not going to church camp this summer."

I helped little Jon climb the monkey bars, steadying him as he scrambled to the top. "Amy-Liz *always* goes to camp. She's never missed a summer. What's up?"

Andie gave Jon's twin, Chris, an under-duck in his swing. "The way I heard it, Amy's dad's been laid off, and they're cutting back on everything."

"Wow," I said softly. "Even Amy's voice lessons?"

"That too."

I felt sorry for Amy-Liz. Sounded like things were perfectly rotten at her house. "Isn't there anything we can do?" I asked, watching closely as Jon jumped down off the bars into the sand below.

Andie frowned. "Like what?"

7

"I just thought we could help. Maybe a bunch of us could pitch in some money."

Andie sat at the bottom of the slide. "You've gotta be kidding, Holly. There's no way Amy-Liz Thompson accepts charity. You oughta know that."

"But," I insisted, "we should try, don't you think?"

Leaning back against the hot slide, Andie shook her head, shielding her eyes from the late afternoon sun. "Nope, it's not a good idea."

"Then . . . *what?* What can we do?"

Unexpectedly, Jon threw a handful of sand at his brother's face. Chris squealed and rubbed his eyes. Andie leaped off the slide and ran to Chris, lifting him from the swing. "No, no, Jon!" she scolded.

"No!" Jon yelled back at her. "No!"

Andie hauled Chris into the house. He kicked against her bare legs as he screamed in pain.

I scolded Jon. "You should never throw sand or dirt in someone's face. You could hurt your brother's eyes."

He squatted in the sand making a circular motion with both hands like he was thinking hard. He wouldn't look at me.

I reached down and patted his arm. "Let's go inside and say sorry to Chris."

Jon stared at the ground, patting the sand with both hands. "No. I make sand cakes. Mushy sand cakes." And he ran to get the hose near the house.

I wanted to say "Forget it, kid," but that's not exactly the best way to get a three-year-old's attention. Little kids always seem to do the exact opposite of what you ask them to. At least that's how it was with the twins. Jon and Chris—just recently out of the terrible twos—had minds of their own. I shouldn't have been surprised. After all, their fourteen-year-old sister was consistently hard-headed.

Jon ran across the length of the yard in his bare feet, talking to himself as he headed for the house. He reached for the outside faucet and it sque-eaked on. Seconds later, water shot out of the hose. I wondered if I should let him make his silly sand cakes, but my mind was really on Andie inside with Chris. She probably needed my help.

"Come here, Jon," I called, but he ignored me. I walked across the yard to turn off the water when a mischievous look slid across his face. That's when he ran toward the nozzle.

So did I.

"Whoa! Stop right there," I shouted, hoping to scare him into submission. But he didn't stop, and both of us ran toward the end of the hose—the hose that lay innocently in the middle of a patch of thick, green grass.

Jon kept running, giggling unmercifully. Fortunately, my legs were longer and my grip tighter.

Man, did he change his tune fast when I threatened him with a cold blast of H_2O.

"Now go over there and turn the water off," I insisted in my most authoritative baby-sitter voice. Holding the hose high, I pressed my thumb against the edge of it. Water gushed out in a fan-like spray.

I inched it closer and closer to the little shrimp's body, while his pleas for mercy rose higher and higher into the warm June breeze.

He hollered, "I'm thorry, Howwy. I'm tho-o-o thorry!"

"You better go tell your brother that." I tried to keep from laughing—wondering how he'd look soaking wet. But being the fabulous baby-sitter I am, I removed my thumb from the spout and let the pressure fizzle out.

Jon stared wide-eyed at the hose. The rushing, roaring Niagara had become a steady stream once again, and Jon's little face looked mighty relieved. "Pwomise you won't spway me?" His lower lip quivered.

I pushed the hose behind my back, feeling bad. "I promise. Now, be a good boy and go turn off the water."

"Uh-huh." He nodded his head sheepishly and turned and ran to the spigot. "It's off!" he shouted, hands in the air as though he'd done something tremendous.

"You're right; it is." I dropped the hose and followed him into the house. How many more willful stand-offs would I encounter before Andie's parents returned home? It was anyone's guess.

As for Andie, I wasn't going to let her talk me out of my fabulous idea. Amy-Liz deserved to go to camp this summer. End of discussion!

TWO

When Jon and I went inside, we found Andie in the kitchen kissing the top of Chris's head. He sat dangling his chubby legs from the kitchen counter. Apparently, Andie had successfully washed out his eyes.

"Everything okay?" I asked.

Andie nodded. "He'll be fine." She eyed Jon, who stood looking down at his toes.

I knelt down beside the little terror and put my arm around him. "Would you like to say something to Chris?"

Jon's head rose slowly. "I'm thorry, Cwis," he said softly.

Andie lifted Chris down off the counter, and Jon put his arms around his twin's neck. "Aw, how sweet," I cooed as the fiercesome twosome kissed and made up.

"Don't hold your breath," Andie whispered to me.

Suddenly, the boys lost their balance and fell onto the floor in a heap of look-alike arms and legs. Giggles too.

Later, we got the twins settled down and cleaned up.

It took some doing even for both Andie and me to get things under control with these live wires. It made me appreciate the fabulous way Andie's mom seemed to handle things every day. And my own mom, who was not only a mother to me and my sister, Carrie, but was now—with her marriage to Uncle Jack last November—stepmother to four of my cousins, too.

While the twins watched a cartoon video in the family room, Andie and I sat on the sofa behind them arguing about Amy-Liz and how to help her.

"C'mon, Andie. It's a great idea," I said.

She shook her head, making her dark curls dance. "How would *you* feel about receiving charity?"

"Charity? Get over it, Andie. Can't you see, Amy's gonna miss out if someone doesn't do something!"

"Yeah, like what?"

Finally, Andie was ready to listen.

I sat up against the sofa, eager to share my very specific, absolutely fabulous idea. "We could have a bake sale."

She cackled. "Coming from someone who hates to bake, that's nuts."

"I don't mind baking. It's cooking I despise."

"Yeah, yeah," she muttered, waving her hand at me like I was suggesting something incredibly outrageous. "So, who're you gonna sell this baked stuff to?"

She'd caught me off guard. "Oh ... people."

"What people?"

I should've known she'd question me every step of the way. Taking a deep breath, I said, "People like neighbors ... uh, and friends. You know, just people."

"Sounds cool." She leaned back against a soft plaid pillow.

Andie was like that. Unpredictable ... and frustrating beyond belief. I never knew what to expect from her.

"So you'll help me then?"

Andie flashed one of her serious stares. "Whatcha gonna bake?"

"What about my Super-Duper Snickerdoodles?"

Andie's eyes brightened. She actually smiled!

"What about you?" I asked. "Don't you have a special Mexican cookie recipe or something?"

Andie gasped playfully, clutching her throat. "You mean our *secret* family recipe? Are you serious?"

I laughed.

"I'd be crazy to let our recipe for polvorones fall into the wrong hands, Holly Meredith." She leaned close, her dark eyes shining. "It's top secret."

"Well, if it's such a big secret, why don't you just make them ... whatever they are. I don't want the recipe anyway."

"You'll want the recipe after you taste them," she replied. "Wait and see." She had a weird dreamy look to her. "So, that settles it. We'll have a bake sale."

I sat up. "Let's start taking orders."

"Not until after my mom gets home."

"I didn't mean right now." I leaned back into the couch and sighed. "Well, thank goodness we're not going to earn Amy's camp money by baby-sitting."

Andie frowned. "What, don't you like my baby brothers?" She picked up the pillow and punched it.

"Course I do, silly. Nothing against your brothers." I paused, thinking how I could get out of this gracefully. Andie wasn't making things very easy for me. "I really love Chris and Jon." I glanced over at them. "You should know that."

"Yeah, right." She sniffed and turned a cold shoulder.

"You know perfectly well I'm serious, Andie. I love helping you baby-sit your brothers." I turned away from her glare, looking over at the darling boys on the floor. Jon sat chewing on his pointer finger, totally entranced with the cartoon characters and their antics. Chris rocked back and forth humming softly to himself, also transfixed on the tube.

"You love getting paid for helping me with my brothers, is more like it." She said it with a straight face and a tinge of anger ... What was going on?

"Andie, I don't get you!" I stood up abruptly.

Jon turned around, startled. "Howwy not go bye-bye," he said, shaking his slobbery finger at me. "Not go."

Andie started to laugh, not her normal cackle, no. This laughter was new. A sort of mid-range laugh

14

with a eerie staccato bounce to it. And it sounded like she wasn't really laughing at all. She had caught me in one of her crazy pretend conflict set-ups. Caught me flat. And what had I done? Fallen for it. I just stood there watching her have her giggle game.

"I really had you . . . Holly . . . I can't believe you fell for . . . this." She stopped laughing long enough to breathe, holding her sides. "How could you think I was actually serious? How could you?"

"Guess I'm gullible, that's all."

"Gullible, mullible," she chanted. More laughter.

Finally, when the giggling ended, Andie settled down to normal—whatever that was—and we planned how to arrange getting the money from our baked-goods sale into the church scholarship fund.

"I'm sure Pastor Rob'll agree to it," I said, thinking how lucky we were to have such a cool youth pastor. "I'll call him first thing tomorrow."

"Make sure he keeps it a secret." She grabbed my arm. "If Amy finds out, the whole thing will backfire."

"I'll tell him to keep it quiet," I promised, amused at her sudden interest. But I was glad to know Andie was supportive of this project, because funding Amy-Liz's camp trip wasn't going to be all that easy.

Getting my hands on Andie's recipe would be a nightmare, probably. She'd said it was top secret. If only she hadn't said it like that.

Now I *knew* I had to have it!

THREE

The next day, even though it was summer vacation, I got up early. Before the sun. I grabbed my journal from its special place in the bottom drawer of my dresser and hurried to my window seat with pen in hand.

Friday, June 17: I can't wait to get started on a fabulous new top-secret project with Andie. If everything goes as planned, we're going to raise zillions for the church camp scholarship fund. Actually, the money's going to Amy-Liz Thompson because her dad's out of work. Since she'd never accept our money any other way, this is a perfect plan!

I can't wait to see her face when she finds out she's going to camp after all!

A quick glance at the calendar told me Andie and I had a lot to do in a short time. The church bus was scheduled to leave for the San Juan mountains next Thursday. That left only five days to take orders, bake goodies, deliver them, and get the money into the church camp account. All without Amy-Liz ever finding out.

Five days!

It would be tricky, but I was confident it could be done. With my organizational skills and Andie's baking ability, not to mention that secret family recipe of hers . . . surely we could pull it off in time.

The first thing I decided to do to expedite matters was call Pastor Rob. I waited till seven o'clock, though. Didn't want to wake him too early. I figured unmarried youth pastors like to sleep in on lazy, summer days.

I tiptoed downstairs to the kitchen, took the portable phone out of its cradle, and hurried to my room. Safe inside, I closed the door. Had to make sure no one overheard this conversation.

The phone rang four times before the answering machine picked it up. After the beep, I left a message and wondered where I'd gotten the crazy notion that single youth pastors slept in on summer mornings. The machine said he was out playing racquetball and could be reached at the church office later in the day.

Ten o'clock to be exact.

I looked at my watch. Yikes! Three hours from now. I let myself freak out for a while about wasting those precious hours, then my thoughts turned to Andie. Maybe I could get things rolling with a quick phone call to her.

Wait . . . knowing Andie, she'd still be in bed. I couldn't risk upsetting her. She might get mad and dump the whole mission in my lap. Without her top-secret recipe!

Snuggling against the pillows in my window seat, I tried to figure out a way to make the time pass more quickly. Goofey, my cat, purred loudly, and I reached for him, holding him close. Minutes dragged as I stared at the clock on my dresser and Goofey lazily washed his paws. Then an idea popped into my head. I should contemplate my life. On paper, of course. The usual way.

I began to write in one of my many spiral notebooks marked "Secret Lists." This one was a skinny red notebook, perfect for making a single list down the left side. Today, I decided, the list would chronicle the major accomplishments of the last school year. Eighth grade.

I, Holly Meredith, age 14 years, 4 months, and 3 days old, with the help of God, accomplished the following:

1. *Passed eighth grade with mostly B's, a few A's, and one C+.*
2. *Played the part of Maria in* The Sound of Music.
3. *Made room in my heart for more than one best friend.*
4. *Survived a huge crush on a teacher . . . Mr. Barnett.*
5. *Learned what true love certainly is not.*
6. *Found out that God waits, sometimes till the very last possible minute, to answer prayers.*
7. *Discovered that having a stepdad can be fabulous.*
8. *Helped pray my father into the family of God.*

9. *Made strides in getting along with my three brousins (cousins turned stepbrothers)— Stan, 16, Phil, 10, and Mark, 8.*
10. *Showed big-sisterly love—most of the time— to Stephie and Carrie. (And may the Lord continue to assist me on this one!!)*

I put my pen down and reread my list. Sounded good. I read it again. Something was definitely missing. Oh yes, I'd sponsored an overseas child.

Number 11. Quickly, I added that to my list.

Leaning against the heart-shaped pillows once again, I thought back over the last school year. Sometimes it was easier, more comfortable, remembering the past than looking ahead to the future. Maybe deep down I understood it, but I shrugged the thought away. Next year—ninth grade—was going to be so different. Too different.

I refused to think about it. After all, nearly the whole summer lay ahead. And in just five days . . . summer camp. A whole week of fun. There would be hiking, swimming, craft classes, horseback riding, camp choir, a talent night. And those romantic campfires!

Our church owned a large mountain property in the San Juan mountains just outside of Ouray, Colorado, three hours from Dressel Hills, our tiny ski town. Ouray, pronounced U-ray, was the perfect place for camp, and I couldn't wait. Besides being a fabulous setting, everyone in our church youth group was going.

Last I'd heard, Jared Wilkins and Danny Myers

were going to share a cabin with Billy Hill, Stan (my stepbrother), and two other guys.

Andie and I, and Paula Miller and her twin, Kayla, would definitely hang together in one cabin. Joy and Shauna, inseparable friends, knew we expected them to join us. Counting Amy-Liz, there would be seven girls crammed into a cabin set up for six girls plus a counselor. It would be tight, but what fun.

Oblivious of the time, I slid off the window seat and stretched for a few minutes. Then I went to get my devotional book and Bible off the lamp table beside my canopy bed. I don't know how long I sat there reading, but suddenly I was aware of footsteps in the hallway. Probably Mom going downstairs to start coffee for Uncle Jack. I leaped off my window seat and opened the bedroom door. "Ps-s-t! Mom?"

The top of her blonde head appeared as she inched backwards up the stairs. "Why are you whispering?" she asked.

"Didn't wanna wake up the whole crew," I said, referring to my five siblings.

Mom smiled, her blue eyes twinkling. "Everyone's already up."

"They are?"

She nodded. "We thought you were sleeping in."

I laughed, glancing over my shoulder at the notebook lying on the window seat beside my cat. "Guess I just got a little carried away."

"Well, come down when you're ready." She buttoned the middle button on her cream-colored duster. "We're having waffles."

"Didn't miss devotions, did I?"

"Uncle Jack left an hour ago," she said, wiggling her fingers into a tiny wave and heading down the steps.

"I'll be right there." I gathered up my pen and the "Secret Lists" notebook, putting it away for safe-keeping. I could almost taste Mom's whole-wheat waffles as I pulled on a pair of pink shorts and T-shirt. Waffles! Now, that's what I call a good way to start the day.

❤   ❤   ❤

After the kitchen was cleaned up with the help of Carrie and Phil—it wasn't my turn, but I pitched in and helped anyway—I ran upstairs to call Andie in the privacy of my room.

"Hey," she answered softly. "It's too early for intelligent conversation, in case you didn't know."

"Just be glad I didn't call you when I first got up," I said, visualizing a disheveled Andie on the other end of the phone. "So you're not officially up yet, huh?"

"You could say that."

"When should I call you back?"

"What's the rush?"

"Well, you know ... remember what we talked about yesterday? About the money thing, for Amy-Liz?"

"That's what you called about?"

"I thought since we only have five days to raise the bucks, we oughta get started."

I could tell Andie wasn't in the mood for fast-moving conversation, let alone actually getting out and knocking on doors, taking orders and stuff like that.

She sighed into the phone. A little too heavily. Was she mad?

"That'll work," she said finally. And then— "You're really serious about this, aren't you?"

I held my breath. She wasn't backing out on me, was she? "Uh, yeah, I'm serious. It's important, you know, for Amy's sake."

Andie yawned into the phone. "I'm on my way. Don't start anything without me."

I pushed the antenna into the phone. I figured she'd be over in an hour or so. Plenty of time to brush my hair and braid it. I reached for the wooden box on top of my dresser. My hair accessories—the colorful scrunchies and tiny hair bands that I used to finish off my long, thick braid—were inside.

Pulling my waist-length hair over my left shoulder, I began brushing. When the braid was secured with a hair band, I went downstairs to the kitchen in search of my recipe box.

Our kitchen was a long, sunny room with the refrigerator and pantry at one end and a built-in corner desk at the other. The pantry was almost what you'd call a walk-in closet, although I couldn't exactly stretch my arms straight out and still close the door. To me, a real pantry was one where a person could actually move around comfortably. Or hide from the world.

As a kid, I had declared this spot the perfect hiding place from my sister, Carrie, now nine. I was much shorter then, and that was long before my parents divorced and Daddy moved to California.

Standing in the doorway, I scanned the shelves for my recipe box. I remembered that it had been an assignment for seventh grade home ec. Probably wouldn't even own one to this day otherwise.

Cooking was Andie's thing, not mine. I'd much rather write stories or read mysteries than keep track of recipes and ingredients. Reflecting on that fact, it suddenly hit me that Andie was right about my plan. Recommending this baking thing really was out of character for me.

Now . . . where was that silly recipe box?

The doorbell rang just as I spotted the yellow-and-brown plaid file box. I reached for the top shelf. "Could someone please let Andie in!" I shouted.

"I'm in," she said, right behind me.

I whirled around, almost dropping the recipe cards. "Don't do that!"

"Do what?"

"Sneak up like that."

Andie snatched the file box out of my hand, grinning. "So this is your famous seventh-grade recipe fiasco!"

"Give me that!" I grabbed for it, but she ran across the kitchen.

"Why'd you always hide this from me?" Her eyes danced mischievously. "You were so-o-o secretive about it."

I could've easily retrieved the box; my arms were much longer than hers, and I was lots taller. "Go ahead, have a look," I said, relinquishing it.

She looked up at me. "You sure?"

"Uh-huh." I nodded, staring out the window acting disinterested. That's when I noticed someone coming through the side yard.

I hurried to the window. I couldn't believe my eyes.

"Lousy timing!" I muttered, aghast. Amy-Liz, wearing one of last year's summer outfits, hurried to the back door. I felt sorry for her—about her father losing his job. And worried, too, that Andie's and my plan would blow up in our faces.

"What's wrong?"

I whispered, "Amy-Liz is here."

Smack! Andie dropped the file box on the island bar. She zipped over to the window.

"You don't think she's heard about our plan, do you?" I said. Without waiting for Andie's response, I turned and snatched my recipe box off the bar, returning it to the pantry.

Andie's eyes were transfixed on the window. Silently, I closed the pantry door behind me. The recipe box was safe. At least for now.

"What'll we do?" I said, tiptoeing to the window beside Andie. "I mean, she might discover the plan, and she won't accept the money if she knows—"

"Relax, Holly," Andie interrupted. And with an impish grin, she turned to look at me. "Just go and open the screen door. Leave the rest to me."

I cast a disapproving glance at my friend as I took baby steps across the kitchen.

Andie shooed me to the back door. "Go on," she whispered. Her eyes danced with mischief.

What *did* Andie have in mind?

24

FOUR

Cautiously, I headed to the door, which stood ajar, letting in the fresh breezes of summer. I unlocked the screen door and let Amy-Liz inside.

"You're late!" Andie told her.

She looked completely startled. "For what?"

Amy-Liz glanced first at me then at Andie, who marched right over to the pantry, flung the door wide, and . . .

Stop! I said with my eyes. Sending messages that way to Andie was a common occurrence. What was she thinking? How could she spoil our fabulous plan?

Andie ignored my facial warnings and brought out my pathetic recipe box, displaying it on the bar. What scheme was she cooking up now?

Andie motioned for Amy-Liz. "Here, pick out something, anything, for Holly to make for supper tonight. She wants to surprise her mother." She glanced over her shoulder and shot me a mighty weird look.

I didn't say anything, mainly because Amy-Liz didn't seem one bit interested in my ratty-looking recipe box.

"Uh, I'm sorry." Amy-Liz backed away from the bar. "I really can't stay. Sorry, Holly,"—she turned to look at me, her blonde curls dangling—"I wish I could help, but I've gotta go. I only stopped by to see if I could borrow some of your music."

Andie smiled, obviously relieved. "Well, you came to the right place, because Holly has tons of it."

I closed the lid on the recipe box and stood in front of it—hiding it—facing the girls. "You may borrow whatever music you'd like," I told Amy-Liz. "Miss Hess let me keep some of the scores from the school musical, you know, just for the summer. I don't think she'd care if you borrowed them."

"Could I?" Amy-Liz seemed delighted.

"Wait here, I'll be right back." I hurried through the dining room to the stairs, leaving the recipe box behind.

When I returned with the music folder, I found Andie and Amy-Liz huddled over the kitchen bar, laughing. They stood up quickly as I came in.

"What's so funny?" I clutched the bulging folder.

"Just this," Andie said, holding up a recipe card. "How do you spell meat loaf?"

I felt humiliation setting in. "Why ... what does it say?" Although I didn't remember much of anything I'd written on those file cards, I did know one thing: part of the home ec. assignment had entailed creating recipes out of thin air. In other words, we were to simply make up whatever we thought would be delicious concoctions.

Andie waved the recipe in my face. "I can tell you one thing—nobody puts baking soda in meat loaf," she announced through a stream of giggles.

Amy-Liz frowned and pursed her lips. "Hey, give her credit for something," she said. "Maybe Holly likes her meat loaf light and fluffy."

I couldn't hold the laughter in. "Yeah, that's it. Puffy meat loaf." Reaching for the file box, I closed the lid. When it was resting safely in my hands, I smiled apologetically. "I think recipe analysis class is over now, girls." I stared at Andie, who caught my meaning instantly. I knew she did because she watched in total silence as I handed Amy-Liz the folder of music.

"Thanks, Holly," Amy said. "This'll keep me busy." She thumbed through the folder without mentioning her family's financial problems or the fact that her voice lessons had been axed. "I'll take good care of this, I promise."

"Have fun with it." I walked her to the back door. "And keep it as long as you want."

"Thanks again . . . and, oh, sorry about your meat loaf recipe."

"No problem."

She waved good-bye. The screen door slapped shut.

"Whew, was that close or what?" Andie muttered when Amy-Liz was gone. "Think she suspected anything?"

"How could she?" I opened my recipe box and flipped through the index cards until I found my Super-Duper Snickerdoodle recipe under the tab marked "cookies and pastries." And not once did Andie comment about the meat loaf—that ridiculous recipe—the rest of the day.

♥   ♥   ♥

Aside from Carrie and Stephie showing up every five minutes to get something to eat, things went rather smoothly. We started work immediately on our money-making project by creating an order form, a kind of chart. Andie's cookie orders went on the left side and mine on the right. When the form was finished, I put my recipe box back in the pantry.

When Carrie and Stephie were safely out of earshot, I called Pastor Rob to tell him our plan. He was delighted with our idea but reminded me of the short time remaining.

That done, Andie and I pranced out the back door eager to take on our first street. My street, Downhill Court.

Probably anyone who saw us standing in front of Miss Hibbard's house next door would have thought we were just two girls out visiting the neighbor lady on a lovely summer day. But it was much more than that. I felt nervous about this whole money-making thing. What if no one wanted to buy our stuff?

"Well, well, if it isn't little Holly Meredith," Miss Hibbard said, peering over her reading glasses. She glanced at Andie. "And who do we have here?" She lifted her head to get just the right angle, finding the bifocal line on her glasses as she reached out to touch Andie's shoulder.

"Aren't you Holly's girlfriend? I believe I do remember the first time the two of you came to visit this old woman. Yes, sir-ee, you were just about this high." She leaned on the screen door with one hand while she held out her other hand, trying to find the correct height in the air.

Andie grinned. "We're taking orders for Snicker-doodles and Mexican wedding cookies today, Miss Hibbard," she said in her most pleasant voice. "You like delicious sweet and nutty treats, right? How many dozen would you like?"

Miss Hibbard gasped. "Dozen? Why, my dear, it's only me all by my little lonesome living here. What could I possibly do with a dozen of anything?"

I sighed. Why did we come here first?

"Well, if you don't mind, Miss Hibbard," Andie continued, "maybe you'd like to purchase a dozen of each and give them away to the children in the neighborhood." Before Miss Hibbard could interrupt, Andie said, "After all, it is for a worthy cause. You see, Holly and I are helping one of our girlfriends go to church camp this summer. Her father—"

"Well, why didn't you say that in the first place, little dear?" And with that old Miss Hibbard disappeared and went to get her purse.

"Why didn't you say that in the first place?" I whispered. "We can't forget this fabulous approach, okay?"

Andie wrinkled up her nose at me playfully. "Well, I think it's about time for you to get your feet wet with this business of door-to-door sales. You may have the privilege of the next house."

"Oh, Andie," I moaned. "You're doing so well. Can't you keep—"

"Here we are, girlies," Miss Hibbard said, flashing a ten-dollar bill as she came to the screen door. "I don't care what it costs, just keep the change. It's for a worthy cause." She adjusted her glasses and looked at us both. "Now, when can I expect those Snicker-doodles?"

My eyes darted to Andie's. Whoops! We hadn't discussed this important angle. "Uh, we'll have them ready by Monday," I said. "Is that all right?"

"Quite all right," the woman said, nodding.

Yes, that'll work, I told myself. *Tomorrow's Saturday—we'll bake up all our orders then—Sunday isn't a good day for deliveries because of church.* Monday was perfect.

"So . . . Monday it is," Andie said, thanking Miss Hibbard for her donation and the order. "Have a lovely weekend, Miss Hibbard."

Together, we scampered down the steps to the sidewalk like schoolgirls on a picnic. We'd made a sale—our very first!

The sun beat down hot on my head as we headed to the next house. I wished I'd worn a hat.

"Okay, it's all yours," Andie reminded me as we made our way to the next house.

"Don't make me do this," I pleaded. "I'll do every-thing else. The clean up, the baking—"

"Not my polvorones, you won't," she said. "That

recipe does not leave my house!" Her eyes twinkled teasingly as I reached for the doorbell.

The neighbor's oldest son showed up at the door wearing his Walkman. I waited for him to remove the plugs from his ears, but he didn't. He just stood there in a half daze caught up in the music or whatever.

"Hey, Bryan," I said, a little too loudly. "Wanna order some—"

"Huh? What'd you say?"

I pointed to his ears.

"Oh, yeah," he mumbled.

I repeated myself, completely forgetting to say the perfect sales pitch that had worked so well with Miss Hibbard.

"Nah, s'too hot for baked stuff," Bryan said and put his earplugs back in.

"See," I told Andie as we reached the sidewalk, "you're much better at this."

"I think I see what you mean." But that isolated incident alone wasn't enough to get me out of doing my share of the sales soliciting. Nope. Andie wasn't one to give up easily.

After an hour of taking orders, we were hungry. Mostly thirsty. We ran back to my house for some lunch and a tall, cold glass of lemonade. Mom had just finished making a pitcherful when we showed up.

"Well, hi there, Andie. Nice to see you," Mom said. Then she asked me, "Have you seen Carrie or Stephie lately?"

"Last I saw them was at breakfast. Why?"

"Well, they were just here a minute ago rummaging through the pantry," she said, looking puzzled.

I looked at Andie, who was frowning like crazy. "Uh-oh," I said. "You don't think—"

"Let's go," Andie said.

"We'll be right back," I called to Mom as I followed Andie through the living room and out the front door.

"What's up?" I asked Andie, letting the door slam accidentally.

"I have a funny feeling we're being watched," she said as we began to scour the neighborhood, "and possibly followed ... if you know what I mean." She sounded like a bonafide detective.

We followed Downhill Court with its bricked sidewalk and tall aspen trees. Turning at the end of the block, we went another whole block before coming to Aspen Street, the main drag in our Colorado ski village.

The elementary school was located on the corner. I knew that my sister, Carrie, and stepsister, Stephie, often hid in the playground area behind the school. To discuss private things, they would say.

I stood in the shade of a clump of aspen trees, searching for signs of them. "See 'em anywhere?"

Andie groaned. "This is so bizarre. Haven't you taught your sisters good manners?"

"What's that supposed to mean?" I glared at her.

"You know. About snooping and stuff."

"Course I have. I threatened both of them with their life last time they sneaked around my room."

Suddenly, I caught sight of Carrie's long blonde ponytail. "Look! There they are. Behind the swings."

There was a long, wooden play area with steps and levels where kids played during recess. Like a fort. I could see Carrie's hair peeking out from behind the wooden slats.

"Let's scare 'em," Andie whispered. "It'll teach them a good lesson."

Perfect!

So, like slithery lizards, we crept across the playground not making a single sound. Quietly, we inched our way. Closer and closer.

I could see Stephanie leaning over, looking at something with Carrie. Her chestnut hair hung around her pixie face as she read out loud. We were only a few feet away from them when Andie spoiled everything by hiccuping.

Carrie turned around, startled.

Andie and I ducked out of sight behind the fort.

"No one's there," Carrie's tiny voice rang out, probably attempting to reassure Stephie.

But Stephie stood up and brushed the sand off her knees. "Something's spooky! I'm getting outta here!"

Another one of Andie's hiccups cut loose. I stood up just as Carrie came around the corner. "Hey! What're you two doing spying on us?" she demanded.

"Well, well. How's it feel?" I glared at the stolen recipe box in her hands.

"Uh . . . it was Stephie's idea, honest," she insisted.

"Well, Stephie's only seven," I said, implying that

she wasn't smart enough to come up with something like that on her own.

"But I can read every word in that recipe box," Stephie said, defending herself innocently.

"Mom's gonna be ticked when she finds out you ripped off my stuff," I said.

Slowly, dramatically, Andie twirled a curl around her finger and moved in for the kill. "Exactly what are you two doing with Holly's recipe box in a school playground, two blocks from home?"

Stephie looked at Carrie and then back at Andie.

"You, there . . . Carrie," Andie said, turning on the not-so-charming side of herself. "Speak up."

Carrie lowered her eyes, avoiding Andie's gaze.

I thought she was going to cry.

"Wait a minute," I intervened. "They can explain all this to Mom later. I'm starved."

"Hold on a minute, Holly," Andie bossed me. She moved closer to Carrie. "I want an answer, little girl, and I want it straight."

Man, did she sound like John Wayne today. Not so much the way she said it, but her words sounded like something out of one of those westerns my oldest stepbrother liked to watch. Except Stan could really turn on the old John Wayne charm when he talked.

Carrie's bottom lip quivered. She was a pro at making it do that. Andie had met her match.

Finally, when Carrie had waited long enough to get the right amount of sympathy kindling inside Andie, she confessed, "We just wanted to do something like you big kids."

"Aha!" Andie shouted. "So you were snooping!"

I was worried that our entire mission was in jeopardy now. "Yo, mate, time out," I said to Andie, giving her the eye.

"All right, you two," Andie said, wagging her pointer finger in Carrie's face. "Don't move. Wait right there!" And we left them looking mighty worried.

Andie and I made our huddle several yards away from the girls. I figured we were far enough from the fort area where Carrie and Stephie stood waiting. No way could they hear us over here.

I spoke first. "Whatever you do, Andie, don't tell them about our project being top-secret."

"Why not? We'll just bribe 'em to keep their mouths shut or something."

"No, it doesn't work that way. We have to make sure they don't tell Amy-Liz what we're doing. It'll spoil everything."

"So don't you at least wanna know how much of our plan they overheard?" Andie hiccuped again.

"Let's just drop it," I suggested. "The more we make of it, the more likely one of them, especially Carrie, might spill the beans at church."

"Okay, have it your way," Andie said, and we grinned at each other, ready to handle the situation in a very diplomatic manner. We turned around ready to reason with the enemy.

Carrie and Stephie were nowhere in sight!

"Why those little . . ." I muttered.

"Look what you did!" Andie wailed.

"I did?"

"Whose idea was it to leave the scene of the crime and huddle up?"

I rolled my eyes. Andie was so good at turning the tables.

"Look, we need to work together on this problem," I said. "Let's try and stick up for each other for once."

That did it.

Andie spun around and stormed off for the fort. She climbed up the chain steps and sat up there sulking. Like a little kid.

"What're you doing?" I called to her.

"You can just count me out of your benevolence project, Holly Meredith!"

I didn't like the sound of this. I sure didn't want to go door-to-door selling my baked wares by myself. Andie was the expert spokesperson, not me. Besides, we didn't have time for this crazy immaturity—summer camp was just five days away!

FIVE

"Fine, have it your way!" I shouted.

I turned around, heading towards the street, trying to look confident. Inside, I was a total coward. In fact, if Andie didn't hurry up and have a change of heart and fall for my bluff and come running, like *now*, I was in big trouble. How could I possibly fill all those orders from this morning's door-to-door work, let alone whatever I would get this afternoon?

The sun was bright. It was a gorgeous day. Perfect for going home, bawling out Carrie for taking my recipe box without asking, giving Stephie the evil eye in hopes that she'd start thinking for herself, and last but not least, heading down the street to peddle my cookies. Alone.

I couldn't worry myself with the problem of making Andie's wedding cookies without her. At least not at the moment. For now, I'd just have to pitch my

Super-Duper Snickerdoodle cookies and hope some-one would buy them.

Over and over, under my breath, I chanted Andie's winning phrases: *This is for a worthy cause. A friend of mine can't afford to go to church camp.*

By the time I reached the front porch of my first prospective buyer, I'd worked up a sweat, not so much from the sun's rays, but from stress.

I rang the doorbell and waited.

Two preschoolers accosted their mother with beggings and pleadings after I told them what I was selling. Now this was exactly the kind of assistance I needed!

The young woman literally had to pull one of the kids off her knee. "Can you wait for just a minute, miss?" she asked.

"No problem." I watched as the kids tore off after her. When she came back with the money for her order, I thanked her and headed to the next house.

Not so bad, I thought as I reached for the next doorbell. By explaining Amy-Liz's dire situation first, I was saving myself time ... and getting the customer's attention.

When I had acquired twenty additional orders, I decided I'd better cool it. If I got too many orders, I wouldn't be able to fill all of them by Monday. Andie and I had racked up seventeen sales earlier this morning. All totaled, I had thirty-seven orders. Nine of them for Andie's polvorones!

I raced home and found Mom and the boys folding laundry downstairs in the family room. Carrie and Stephie were hustling piles of clean clothing off to the respective bedrooms.

Maybe I'll get Mom to help me, I thought. But how to approach her . . . and when? Since becoming step-mom to four kids, she was lucky to have a couple free minutes in her day. I really didn't want to bother her with my problems.

And Andie? Well, I could hardly believe it. She'd actually given in to her madness and stayed angry this time. All afternoon!

I went to my room, straightened it up a bit, and then wrote in my journal. *Friday afternoon, June 17th: I can't figure Andie out anymore. She's really changing. I wonder sometimes if we aren't growing in different directions. I guess it's really no one's fault, but still, it feels real lousy.*

I still can't understand why she didn't want to follow through with my fund-raiser for Amy-Liz. And after all the work she did with me this morning. I know she likes Amy-Liz as much as I do. All I can say is—maybe her heart just isn't in it. Well, nothing's going to stop me! Not now . . . not ever!

Closing my diary, I glanced at the list of orders.

I hadn't taken any orders for Andie's recipe this afternoon. Still, I had tons of work ahead of me. I nearly shook thinking about coming up with twenty dozen Snickerdoodles by Monday. Not to mention the nine dozen—that's one hundred and eight—polvorones which I had no idea how to make!

"Lord, help!" I whispered. "This is for a very worthy cause."

After supper, the phone rang. I almost dropped the phone when I heard Andie's voice.

"How'd you do?" she asked.

"How'd I do what?"

"You know, the orders?" she said. "You did go back out this afternoon, didn't you?"

Not to be pushed into a corner, I said, "Hold just a minute, Andie," and went to the kitchen to get a drink of water. A long, very slow one.

"What's going on?" she asked when I came back to the phone.

"What do you mean?"

"C'mon, Holly, don't play games with me. I've got something very cool to tell you."

I tried to sound disinterested. "Like what?"

"You won't believe it, girl," she went on like she was really excited. "After you left, I went around to a bunch of houses, and I just got done counting my orders."

"Wait a minute, did you say—"

"You heard right," she said. "I rounded up twenty dozen orders for Mexican wedding cookies!"

I gasped. "You did what?"

She was laughing hysterically. "We're really in business now!"

"No kidding." Wow, what a bizarre turn of events. Maybe Andie wasn't changing so much after all!

"So where do you wanna do the baking?" she asked. "My house or yours?"

"Sounds like a project bigger than us both," I said, suddenly feeling a little lightheaded and over-whelmed. I could just see us trying to get things

40

done at her house with little Chris and Jon running around, snatching cookies off the table. And here? Well, it could only work if Uncle Jack took all the kids out of the house and left Mom home to help bake.

"I say we grab the Miller twins and some other girls in the youth group and bake at the church," she suggested. "What do you think?"

It was nice hearing Andie ask me for my opinion for a change. Actually, I was still too stunned to comment. I mean, just five minutes ago I was convinced that Andie had dumped the entire project!

"Well?" she persisted. "Any ideas?"

"Short of hiring out some help, we don't have much choice, do we?" I sighed. "The church kitchen is the perfect place.... How many dozen did you say again?"

Andie giggled. "It's okay, Holly, really. I think we'll probably end up funding more than one needy kid with the proceeds from this project."

"You're right." We said good-bye and I hung up the phone. Whew—what a day tomorrow was going to be!

❤   ❤   ❤

Not only did Paula and Kayla Miller show up to help, their mother came along, too. So did Shauna, Joy, and three other girls. Even Mrs. Martinez, Andie's mom, came to help supervise for a while.

When it came time to make Andie's recipe, she acted as though none of us should even see the

41

recipe card. "It's been passed down for three genera-
tions," she bragged.

"Andrea, for goodness' sake!" her mother said,
frowning.

I sneaked over when Andie wasn't looking and
saw part of the ingredients. "Hmm, yummy," I said,
reciting the first three items on Andie's index card.

"Holly!" She spun around. "Keep away!"

Her mom shook her head as she chopped away at
a pile of pecans. "Share the recipe, will ya?"

Andie stuck the recipe down her blouse, grinning.

"Aw, Andie, just *one* little peek?" I pleaded. "Ple-e-
ase?"

The Miller twins and Shauna inched closer, slowly
surrounding Andie.

"What shall we do to bribe her?" I asked.

"Girls, girls!" Mrs. Miller called to all of us. "We
have lots of work to do. Better get started."

"Call your daughters off me!" Andie hollered, now
giggling.

"We'll leave you alone if you let us see the recipe
for thirty seconds," Paula suggested.

"Ten!" Andie said, holding her hands against her
chest.

"That's not even long enough to focus," I said.

"Okay, okay." Andie finally gave in. "Twenty seconds." She pulled the recipe file card out of her
blouse—holding it in front of her while she counted
out loud.

"Looks easy enough to me," I said, playing it
down in hopes of defusing the situation.

"Anybody can bake these!" Kayla insisted. "What's the big deal?"

Andie's face broke into a broad smile. "Wait'll you bite into one! Just wait!"

We set to work sifting flour, mixing confectioner's sugar, and mashing butter.

Stan stopped by at lunchtime with sandwiches for everyone made by Mom. Wow, what an angel! (Mom, not Stan, although sometimes he could qualify, I guess.)

Andie started talking about delivering the orders.

"We haven't really worked out all the details yet," she said, glancing at me for moral support.

I nodded. Andie was right. This thing had mushroomed into an monstrous mission!

Then, out of the blue, Stan offered to drive us around Dressel Hills on Monday and Tuesday. Andie said she had so many orders, we might need two days for the deliveries.

"That'll be perfect," I said, giving Stan a playful hug before I went back to chopping pecans with Andie's mom.

"Hey, what about Billy and Danny?" Stan suggested. "Betcha they'd help."

Paula smiled at her twin.

"Good idea," Kayla said.

"Then it's settled," I said, explaining where we'd meet and who would do what.

Paula and Kayla chattered about Billy and Danny and what an asset to this project they'd be. "I'll call Billy right now," Paula said, reaching for the phone.

"Remember to tell him to keep things quiet," I said in her ear. "This can't get back to Amy-Liz."

Paula nodded her head. "Oh, you don't have to worry. Billy can keep a secret."

It was interesting watching the relationships evolve between Paula and Billy and Kayla and Danny. Towards the end of school the foursome had been seen double-dating around town. I'd seen them at our favorite hangout, the Soda Straw, several times.

I honestly felt good seeing the Miller twins, who were still rather new to Dressel Hills, hanging out with some of the church guys around here. And, surprisingly enough, Danny seemed to be making his friendship with Kayla work. As far as I could tell, there'd been no evidence of Bible thumping yet. Danny had a tendency to get preachy with his friends, something that became intolerable during the short time he and I were together.

It really didn't bother me seeing him with someone new. Danny Myers and I were history as far as romance goes, and I was sure he felt the same.

The baking was finished by suppertime thanks to all our fabulous help—an assembly line of workers. We'd even made extra cookies for the fun of it and shared them all around before everyone left. And Andie wasn't kidding. Those polvorones were out of this world.

Sunday school and morning and evening services came and went, and, miraculously, Amy-Liz was still completely in the dark about our secret project. Andie and I were giddy with excitement as we anticipated the many deliveries we'd be making.

"It's so cool, this whole thing," Andie said to me as we sipped orange juice on my front-porch swing early Monday morning. "I'm glad you thought of doing it."

"What a job, though," I said, reaching for a cream-filled donut. "I hope I never see another Snickerdoodle for as long as I live."

She laughed. "Ditto for polvorones."

We sat around relaxing as we waited for Stan to get back from downtown. Uncle Jack had given Stan permission to drive him to work so we'd have the van for our deliveries. So far, Stan was the only guy in the youth group with a driver's license. It was perfect, because not only was Stan Patterson my stepbrother, but he was also Andie's boyfriend. Between the two of us, we could rope him into just about anything these days.

Andie and I laughed about it. "We've got Stan wrapped around both our little fingers," I said, holding my hand up.

She glanced at her watch. "Hey, where is he?"

"Give him time," I said. "You know how guys are. He probably dropped Uncle Jack off at the office and decided to drag Main Street awhile."

"Is he wearing a watch?" Andie asked.

"Even if he isn't, there's one on the dash."

"Yeah," Andie said softly. "So what's keeping him?"

I shrugged my shoulders and reached up to

tighten the purple scrunchie holding my ponytail. "He'll be here sooner or later; you'll see."

But at nine-thirty, Stan still hadn't shown up.

"What'll we do?" Andie moaned. "If we don't get started soon, we'll never get done." She studied her list with all the names and addresses. "It'll take us forever."

I hadn't counted on Stan being this late. Surely he hadn't gone off fishing or something else with his buddies. I got off the porch swing and went inside.

"Mom!"

When she didn't appear instantly, I went downstairs and checked the laundry room.

The house was quiet. Too quiet.

Quickly, I ran upstairs. She wasn't in her room. Not in any of the kids' rooms either. I opened the door to Carrie and Stephie's bedroom. Both of them were sound asleep.

"That's strange," I said, closing their door. "Mom's gotta be around here somewhere."

Determined to locate her, I went back downstairs, through the kitchen, and out to the new addition. Phil and Mark were also sleeping when I tiptoed into their room.

Stan's room, however, was alive with sound. I dashed into his bedroom, through the maze of car mechanics magazines and a pile of underwear, and turned off his radio. Then I glanced around, looking for clues as to his whereabouts.

I knew he'd be furious if he found out I had rummaged through the junk on his dresser. But when I saw the note with Jared Wilkins' phone number and the words: *Video arcade—tomorrow*, I leaped for joy. Of course, Stan was probably thinking a couple rounds at the old arcade downtown wouldn't hurt. There'd be plenty of time before driving Holly and her friends all over town.

That's what he thought! Now his irresponsibility had put us behind by a whole hour. How rude!

Guys!

SIX

When I told Andie the news, she scrunched up her face. "Well, that's easy enough," she said. "We'll just call the arcade and roust him outta there."

I could see it now, the place crammed to the seams with kids exhibiting that glazed-over look in their eyes, while the phone rang off the hook. If there even was a phone!

Andie stood up, empty donut plate in hand, and headed for the kitchen. "So where's your phone book?"

"Where's my mom is a better question." I told her how I'd searched the house and found nothing but sleeping children everywhere.

"Maybe she went for a walk."

"Maybe."

Andie put her plate in the sink while I dragged the phone book out from the drawer. "I'll look it up," Andie offered.

I handed her the phone book. "Be my guest."

"Hmm, let's see . . ." She flipped through the book, found her place, and slid her finger down the page. "This oughta be it."

I pressed the numbers while she called them out. And just as I had anticipated, the phone rang and rang. And rang.

No one even bothered to set foot outside their individual game-world. Reality-based worlds such as telephones and girls waiting for promises to be kept had been lost in the mind-numbing maze of sight and sound and the challenge of defeating monsters. What could be more important, after all?

"Okay, now what?" Andie closed the phone book and placed it on the bar.

"Don't ask me." I stared at the flecks of gold in the counter top. "This is so typical," I muttered. "You just can't count on guys!"

Andie ran her fingers through her short, curly locks. "Okay, calm down." She was thinking it through. "If we hop the bus and go downtown—"

I sighed. "That'll take too much time. We've gotta think of another way."

She pulled out a bar stool and sat down, leaning her elbows on the bar. "So, what's your plan?" She stared at me.

I'd thought of a back-up plan, all right, but I knew Andie wouldn't be thrilled about it. Standing up, I took a deep breath. "We could make our own deliveries."

"Like how?"

"With a little help from Carrie and Stephie."

She pulled on the sleeve of her T-shirt. "You're joking, right?"

"Ever hear of wagons?"

She pretended to fall off the bar stool. "Wagons? Are you crazy, Meredith? Do you know how long it's gonna take to pull loaded wagons around to all those houses?"

"Better than nothing," I said.

We threw around the idea some more.

"Hey, wait a minute," she said. "Whatever happened to Billy and Danny helping us? Weren't they supposed to show up today, too?"

"You're right." I drank the rest of my orange juice. "Paula called Billy from the church on Saturday, remember?"

She nodded. "Maybe Stan was supposed to pick them up."

"You know how guys are." It was true. Right now—when they were supposed to be over here assisting us with our noble mission—Stan, Billy, and maybe even Danny were probably shooting the breeze under the hood of a car somewhere. Or hanging out at that ridiculous arcade with Jared!

Finally, after another glass of cold orange juice, Andie gave in. "If this is the best we can do, let's do it." She mumbled something pretty nasty about Stan—and guys in general—before helping me get two red wagons down off their hooks in the garage. We loaded them carefully with stacked boxes of cookies.

I amazed myself. It actually looked like we knew what we were doing as we wheeled our goods down the driveway and onto the bricked sidewalks of Downhill Court. Andie continually checked our lists as we made one delivery after another. One customer wasn't home, so we put the orders inside the screen door. The main door behind it bumped open, revealing a snoring man on the living room floor!

Later, we encountered a bulldog running loose in the neighborhood and freaked out for awhile. Andie suggested we feed him a box of cookies—to get the fierce look off his forbidding face. I said we couldn't spare any and suggested we ignore him. And we did ... for three blocks! Finally, the problem was solved when we spotted my mom chatting with a neighbor down the street. She had been walking and said she'd lost track of time. Like someone else we knew!

"Will you take this dog home for us?" I whined, dumping my woes on her—about Stan not showing up, and about the heat, and this miserable beast following us around.

She called to the ferocious fellow. He must've sensed the nurturing nature in her and went right to her. Mom looked at his collar, locating his home address and phone number. "I'll call the owner," she said, heading into the neighbor's house.

"I hope Mom gets on Stan's case for not showing up," I mumbled to Andie, wiping the sweat off my face.

But the worst thing happened hours later when Andie and I were in the middle of our own personal heat strokes.

Jared Wilkins rode by on his bike. He snickered.

"Well, whaddaya know—it's the little red wagon brigade!"

"Beat it," Andie shouted. "It's all your fault."

"Yeah," I said, fanning myself with my hand. "Yours and Stan's."

Jared looked incredulous. "I don't get it. Could you two be a tad more specific?"

I spun around, dropping the handle on my wagon. "You spent the morning with Stan, right?" I said, exasperated.

He shook his head.

"At the arcade, remember?"

"I just got up." He ran his fingers through his hair as he thought it over. "Hey, wait a minute, I was supposed to meet Stan—downtown." He turned and smiled. "Hey, thanks, Holly. Almost forgot."

I called after him frantically, but he kept pedaling down the street in the direction of downtown.

"What a nightmare!" I said.

I turned around to see Andie opening one of the boxes, searching for eats. "I don't know about you," she said, "but I'm going to die right now if I don't grab a bite."

I pulled her away from the opened box. "No, no, you can't eat up our orders. If you're that hungry, let's go back home."

She looked up at me, eyes filled with frustration. "Here's the deal," she said, clutching her throat for effect. "If I leave now and take a break, you'll never, I repeat, never get me back out here in this heat again today."

"But what about our customers? We promised!"

"Promises are made to be broken—isn't that what Stan and the rest of the guys did to us?"

I could see she was on the point of collapse. It was hot. So hot that I wished my hair was shorter instead of waist length. Thank goodness for one fat braid on a day like this.

"Look, Andie," I said. "I know it's hot, and you're wiped out, but we've gotta finish this. Here, I'll take your orders while you go back to my house for lunch. Just leave your wagon parked here and I'll keep working."

"What about you?" She wiped the perspiration off her neck with a tissue.

"I'll manage. Besides Mom should be home by now. Maybe she'll bring you back with something to eat and drink."

Andie huffed her response.

I could see this was asking too much. "Okay, okay, just fill up two sports bottles with ice water. That'll work. Oh, and bring the sunscreen."

She smiled weakly. "You're really something, Holly, in case you didn't know it."

I wanted to say yes, I knew. After all, nobody else in their right mind was out here in these blazing temperatures without a canteen of water or ice cold pop, getting sun-fried.

"Hurry home," I called to her as I made my way up a set of very familiar steps carrying two square boxes. One very frazzled mom and two clingy preschoolers came to the door.

The thrill of surprising Amy-Liz with a camp scholarship began to crowd out a zillion negative things such as hot temperatures, a parched tongue, and a growling stomach. Either that or my brain was cooked and I didn't know it.

Anyway, I was back on track—I kept telling myself—forcing polite smiles for the customers as I made each delivery, pushing myself onward.

One more block. Just one more . . .

And at the end of that block I repeated the same thing again. Over and over, I pushed doorbells, keeping my promise to make the deliveries. No one would've even remotely suspected that I was secretly dying for the moment when Stan or Mom would pull up in our gloriously air-conditioned van.

Just when I thought I'd conquered and suppressed the desperate urge for a cool, refreshing drink, some guy came walking his white toy poodle, guzzling a can of pop. He must've seen my desperation as I stared longingly at the pop, because he stopped and started talking to me.

"Man, you're wiped out," he said.

I stumbled over to an aspen tree. I felt dizzy as I sat down, leaning my head against the trunk's white bark.

Unexpectedly, he held out his can of what I thought was icy, cold pop. "Here, want some V–8?"

In spite of my thirst, I didn't feel comfortable drinking after a complete stranger. Besides, a yucky vegetable drink made with tomatoes and celery and other hidden healthy stuff didn't exactly sound thirst quenching. And after being held in the sweaty palm of some stranger, the juice was probably lukewarm and congealing.

Guys!

I shook my head and declined, which was probably a big mistake, but at this point, I didn't care.

"Thanks anyway," I whispered.

He shrugged, said something to his dog, and off they went.

As I sat beneath the aspen trees, my tongue thick with thirst, I clearly realized why the rich man in the Bible had pleaded with Lazarus to cool his tongue with a single drop of water. Vegetable juice just didn't cut it!

Now I'm not saying Dressel Hills, Colorado is like hell in any sense of the word. It's just this heat . . . this unbearable heat . . . this . . .

I closed my eyes, praying for relief, not caring about the wagon still half filled with cookies waiting to be delivered. All I could think about was how hot and thirsty I was.

Until now, I'd never really thought about hell. Our pastor's sermons weren't hell-bent like some ministers' sermons. In fact, he hardly ever mentioned the place. For some reason, our pastor was more into heavenly things when it came to preaching sermons. Maybe he thought people ought to choose God's Son out of a desire for divine, unconditional love, not because they were scared silly. Or . . . maybe that wasn't the reason at all. Maybe it was a lot more fun to preach about a perfect, fabulous place created by our heavenly Father, than a hot, miserable pit prepared for the devil and his angels.

"Hot . . . pit," I muttered, fanning my face with my limp hand. "Horrible."

Waves of heat surrounded me. I sank into them ...

"Holly-Heart." A familiar voice spoke my name.

I was too weak to respond, but I felt a cool palm against my feverish brow. Lightly, gently, she pushed back my bangs and the touch of her hand made my eyes flutter open.

"Oh, Mom ... it's you."

Nearly incoherent, I thought I'd died and gone to heaven. The way her hand felt against my forehead—like the brush of an angel's wing. And then the sudden stream of cool water on my tongue. It was heaven all right. Heaven on earth.

"Andie, help me get her into the van," I heard Mom say. She said it with the sweetness of one who could be trusted to take care of me. Mom was like that. I could count on her. Unlike some boys I knew.

I strained to hear her voice. But it came and went like a poor phone connection.

"Holly, can ... you hear ... me?"

I tried to let her know I could, but my voice wasn't working. Nothing was.

I heard her talking to me again, but she sounded frightfully distant. As hard as I tried, I knew in my foggy state her voice was fading fast.

And then ... it was gone.

SEVEN

I drifted in and out, slightly aware of a plastic straw being propped between my parched lips. "Here, try to take a sip, Holly."

Straining to look up at the source of the voice, I was surprised to see Stan. Where had he come from? I sipped some cool water as I tried to get my bearings.

"Next time, why don't you use your brain and come in when it gets too hot," he scolded.

"Wha-at?" I mumbled drowsily, looking around. Strange.

I found myself lying on the living room sofa. "Where's Mom?" I asked, pushing stray strands of hair away from my face.

Stan squatted beside me. "She and Andie are out delivering cookies."

I sighed. "What time is it?"

He glanced at his watch. "Twelve-thirty. Why?"

"Guess I oughta eat something."

57

"You're right, you should." He got up and hurried off to the kitchen like he was the big man in charge.

He shuffled around with utensils and things, and that's when I decided he should have to make my lunch every single day for the rest of the summer. I wanted to punish him for the miserable way he'd abandoned us this morning.

While I waited for lunch, I thought about asking him why he hadn't shown up earlier. But I decided it was the wrong time. I wouldn't bring it up. Instead, I'd play the noble martyr and make him feel like the heel he was.

Stan himself brought up the subject when he returned, balancing a paper plate filled with chips and a tuna sandwich. "Uh, sorry about this morning," he said rather feebly, handing me the lunch. "Got sidetracked a little."

"No problem," I said airily, avoiding his gaze. I picked at the chips, fuming inside.

"I said I was sorry ... what do you want me to do, bleed?"

Then I blurted out what I didn't want to say. "Well, if you'd helped us like you promised, instead of spacing out at the arcade, I wouldn't be suffering right now, you know."

There. I'd said it.

Silence reigned for a moment. Then he got up and started to walk away. "Look, girl, from now on make your plans without me," he sneered.

I nearly choked. "It was your idea to help make deliveries, remember?"

His only response to that nasty note of truth was

58

silence. Some stepbrother he was. But I figured it was par for the course. After all, he couldn't help it; he was a guy!

Much later, when Mom and Andie arrived, I was still peeved at the way the day had turned out. I wasn't very good company. Not for Andie, not for anyone. And my sunburn felt hotter than ever.

When Mom cornered Stan in the kitchen, I heard every word between them. "I want you to get out there and finish up those deliveries for Holly," she said sternly. "And when you get back from camp, you will be grounded for one week."

"But Mom," he whined. He sounded just like Carrie and Stephie.

I snickered, scrunching down in the sofa next to Andie.

Mom continued, "You have an obligation to fulfill your promise to your sister and Andie." She wasn't budging on this one, and I secretly applauded. "Now, I don't want to hear anything more out of you, or I'll add another day to your grounding."

When the kitchen encounter was over, Stan turned things around and acted like some kind of hero. Probably for Andie's benefit. Not for mine. I couldn't care less about his sudden change of attitude except that it meant our baked goods would get to our customers as promised.

My veins pulsed with anger. The idea to raise money for Amy-Liz Thompson had been my idea. Now Stan was waving like a valiant soldier before he headed out the door to make the rest of our deliveries. His schizoid behavior was back!

"Who does he think he is?" Andie said as we watched from the living room window.

I scowled at Stan even though he couldn't see me. "He's so-o disgusting."

"Worse," Andie hissed.

I turned to look at her. "You two still going out?"

"Barely." She shrugged flippantly. "All he wants to do is play those mindless arcade games and brag about 'the virtues of virtual reality.' I'm really wondering whether it's worth being tied down to a guy like that."

"Especially since camp's almost here." I giggled, starting to feel much better just thinking about the possibility of the male options at Camp Ouray.

"I know what you mean," Andie agreed.

Carrie and Stephie showed up just then. "How much money did you guys make?" Carrie asked, eyeing the leather money pouch Uncle Jack had loaned us for the occasion.

"Let's count it," Andie said with a sparkle in her smile.

"Well, well," I said to Andie, "it sounds like you're actually excited about this project after all." After my words slipped out, I realized how insinuating they sounded.

"Don't give me that," she shot back. "Just because I didn't nearly sacrifice my life and die on the blazing sidewalks of Dressel Hills, doesn't mean I didn't do my part!"

"Okay, okay," I said, dumping the dollars out on the coffee table. I handed the loose change to Carrie and Stephie, who spread it on the living room carpet and took turns counting it.

Together, the four of us tallied up the proceeds. By the time we subtracted the money for all the ingredients and the boxes we had to buy at the uptown baker, there was enough money to send not only Amy-Liz to church camp, but three more kids!

That, of course, is when Carrie got the not-so-bright idea to pass herself off as a teenager. "I could go to youth camp, don'tcha think?" She pulled her hair up and strutted around the room.

"I don't think so," Andie sang. "Besides, you don't wanna go to camp—there'll be boys there!"

Carrie sassed back, "Maybe that's why I wanna go."

"Well, you'll just have to wait," Andie replied quickly. "Pastor Rob wants kids to be thirteen before they join youth group."

Carrie moaned, then muttered something about having four long years ahead of her.

"What's your hurry?" I asked, remembering Mom's response to me when I was twelve.

Carrie sat on the floor, letting her blonde hair cascade down her back. "There's a cute boy in the group, that's all."

I gasped. "You're kidding, right?"

"Nope," she said with a straight face. "I'm ready to go out."

"Better not let Mom hear you say that," I told her.

"Besides," Andie piped up, "boys aren't as cool as you think." She looked at me with her all-knowing grin. "Right, Holly?"

After a zillion and one hints, Carrie and Stephie finally left the room so Andie and I could talk privately. Not only were we thinking identical thoughts where the guys were concerned, her finger was doing its twirly thing with her curls, which meant one thing: the church youth male population was in *big* trouble!

❤   ❤   ❤

The following morning, I boarded the city bus, the money pouch safely in hand. Andie and I had agreed to meet the youth pastor at the church. He would see to it that the money we'd earned got to the church treasurer in plenty of time. Then he would notify Amy-Liz and her folks about the church scholarship.

Andie joined me several blocks down. The minute she got on, I could tell by her face that she had bad news.

"What's up?" I asked.

She bounced into the seat. "More boy trouble!" Then she proceeded to tell me the latest about Paula Miller's hassles with her boyfriend, Billy Hill. "She says he's forgetting to show up for dates, and other bad stuff."

"How rude!"

"I know it," she said. "But the worst thing is he's paying more attention to her twin than to her."

"Sounds perfectly awful," I said.

"Wanna know my theory?" She frowned. "The guys around here are simply spoiled rotten. Spoiled brats—that's what."

"But Billy Hill ... I thought—"

"Think again. He's turning out to be just like the others." She lowered her voice. "And just for the record, I broke up with Stan last night. For leaving us in the lurch yesterday. And for making you faint dead away from heat stroke."

I stared at Andie, shocked. "You're kidding! I *thought* he was hoarding the phone too long last night."

She shrugged, acting like she didn't care. But her words told another story. "Did he say anything?" she said, almost too casually.

"What do you care?" I teased. "You broke up, right?"

She sighed. "Oh, I don't know. Sometimes it's nice to know the other person feels some of the pain, too." She sat up straight and as tall as she could for being inches under five feet. One thing for sure, though, she looked fired up and determined to follow through with the breakup.

I tried to encourage her. "It's really much better this way. You need to be available—without a boyfriend—when camp starts. You just never know who might show up."

"Maybe . . ." She took a deep breath. The breakup between her and Stan wasn't quite as easy as she was trying to let on.

"Sounds to me like the whole youth group's falling apart," I said, "at least in the romance department."

Andie nodded pensively, and I knew by her silence she wasn't wild about discussing anything pertaining to guys.

♥   ♥   ♥

When the church came into view, we got off the bus. I clutched my money pouch as we strolled up the sidewalk to the church.

At the corner, waiting to cross the street, we spotted Kayla Miller, Paula's twin. Instead of looking fabulous, as usual, she looked rather pathetic. And even though I'd once used "pathetic" to describe Paula, this time I meant the word in a completely different way. Something was very wrong with Kayla.

It didn't take long for Andie to notice. "Hi," she said, giving me a quick nod of her head when Kayla wasn't looking. The gesture meant we should hang around and talk. Cheer her up.

"Well, hello," Kayla said, forcing a smile. "Are you pleased with the outcome of your pastry sales?"

The Miller twins always talked like they were fresh out of another century. But Andie and I were used to it; it was no big deal anymore.

"Fabulous results," I responded, more interested in finding out why she had wet mascara streaks down her usually perfect made-up face. "Are you okay?"

Kayla reached for her shoulder bag and groped for a tissue. "Danny's completely unreasonable," she sobbed.

I might've predicted she and Danny Myers would end up like this. "So, which chapter and verse did he quote this time?" I blurted out.

She actually looked a bit stunned, but after she blew her nose she made no comment, so I didn't push for details. If she didn't want to talk about it, fine. It was her choice. Besides, she might get the wrong idea if I pursued the matter, especially since Danny and I had gone out before.

Kayla's face said far more than a batch of angry words. Her attitude toward Danny, and guys in general, permeated the air. She was one more innocent victim of some unthinking guy's lousy behavior.

Andie finally spoke up. "So did you call it quits?"

"Absolutely," Kayla said between nose blowing and eye patting.

"Well ... join the club," Andie said, not pompously, but almost militantly.

"You, too?" Kayla said.

Andie nodded. "I think it's time for a major change around here."

I registered exactly what she was thinking. "No kidding," I said, thinking of yesterday's lineup of miserable males: Stan's irresponsible attitude, Jared's glib "little red wagon" comment, and that goofy guy with the can of tepid V–8.

Kayla dabbed her tissue up and down her cheeks. "It sounds to me as though too many of us have suffered the ill effects of having been involved in romantic situations," she said.

We agreed, consoling her by inviting her to accompany us to the church. When she'd composed herself, we walked up the steps to the main doors, camp scholarship money in hand.

Pushing open the church door, we headed inside like three musketeers. Down the hall, past the senior pastor's office suite and the secretarial offices, to Pastor Rob's little home-away-from-home.

He smiled, looking up from his desk as the three of us came breezing in. "G'morning, girls."

He looked relaxed in light gray casual slacks and a striped golf shirt. "Whoa, somebody's got a sunburn," he said, looking at me.

"For a very good cause," I said placing the camp money proudly in front of him on his desk.

"Thanks for your hard work," he said. "I know Amy-Liz will appreciate this."

I spoke up. "But you can't tell her, okay?"

"I won't breathe a word." He grinned.

The feeling I had as we skipped down the front steps of the church was excitement, pure and simple. Amy-Liz was going to camp!

EIGHT

Thursday, June 23rd: Yikes! It's five in the morning! I can't believe I'm writing this early. It feels more like the middle of the night than the crack of dawn. This'll be the last time I write for one whole week!

I wish I could take my journal along, but it's totally impossible—someone could find it and read it. No sense risking that. Besides I'll be too busy.

I looked at my watch. Time to shower and get dressed for the day. Reluctantly, I held my journal, cradling it in my arms.

Seven days. A painfully long time to go without writing. Somewhat reverently, I placed my pen and journal back in my bottom dresser drawer. But before I finished packing, I slipped a blank spiral notebook in my overnight bag. Just in case . . .

♥   ♥   ♥

The church parking lot was crowded with parents and kids when we arrived. Actually, the place was totally tumultuous. I couldn't remember seeing so many bags of luggage piled up, except maybe during choir tour last year.

The Miller's van took forever to unload. Looked like Paula and Kayla had brought along their entire wardrobe and eight sets of shoe boxes to boot!

Danny Myers was carrying a mountain of books, and I was sure several of them were Bibles. I wondered if Pastor Rob was going to have Danny lead some of our devotions. He was good at it, all right. If only he could learn to temper his Scripture quoting away from the pulpit.

Amy-Liz and her friends, Shauna and Joy, stood around talking with each other's parents. I noticed the brightly colored socks Amy wore. Always wore. Neon green today. The hot socks were her fashion signature. It was a way to personalize her wardrobe. I was thrilled—she was coming to camp!

I rushed over to her. "Hi, Amy!"

She smiled. "I can't believe this. I'm really here!"

"I'm *really* glad you're going. We'll have a riot in our cabin!"

After we said good-bye to our bleary-eyed moms and dads, Andie, Paula, Kayla, and I found seats together on the bus. We settled in for a three-hour drive to Camp Ouray, smack in the middle of the rugged San Juan mountains of southwestern Colorado.

Unlike the wild and crazy camp bus scenes so often depicted in books and movies, our bus ride was fairly sane. Most the guys on board had wadded up a pillow and dozed off. I could see Jared and Stan toward the back of the bus sawing logs. Danny and Billy Hill were out of it, too.

Amy-Liz sat toward the front with Shauna and Joy singing songs in harmony from *The Sound of Music*. I watched Amy's face as she sang one of Maria's songs, obviously ecstatic about going to camp. Tiny tears of joy came to my eyes, but I brushed them away before anyone noticed.

On our church bus trips, girls were supposed to sit with girls, and guys with guys. So everywhere the girls sat, you could see two heads stuck close together, either whispering or giggling. A few of the guys, those who were not already asleep, were already munching down on snacks.

Andie, Kayla, Paula, and I passed the time by discussing everything from how to keep sneakers deodorized with sprinkles of baking soda to how many outfits we'd packed for camp.

"How many nice outfits did you bring?" Paula asked me.

"Two."

"That's all?" Kayla looked dumbfounded.

I explained my strategy. "I read a book once about packing light and still being able to bring along lots of different looks."

"Like how?" Kayla chirped in disbelief.

"The trick is to layer, you know, like for weather changes and stuff. You never know what might happen in those ominous San Juan mountains," I answered.

Kayla looked worried. This was her first trip to Ouray. "What do you mean, ominous?"

"For one thing, lightning storms can come up out of nowhere, and sunburn is always a problem in such high altitude," I said, remembering my own bout with intense heat three days ago. "And . . . it's even possible to encounter a freak blizzard this time of year."

Andie groaned. "Oh, spare me. Let's not talk about snow storms."

Paula nodded sympathetically. "You must be thinking about the night we spent at school in that blizzard last March."

"Uh-huh," Andie said, glancing at me.

I remembered the blizzard. People had called it the storm of the decade. But it wasn't the lousy weather that stuck in my mind. Jared Wilkins had shown his true colors that night, and we ended up having a terrible argument. The worst ever. Trapped inside the school with the wind howling and the snow falling, we'd called it quits. Definitely forever.

Andie must've sensed my reminiscing. "So back to the wardrobe thing," she prompted me. "Tell us more."

I shifted gears mentally, letting the image of Jared and me breaking up fade a bit before continuing. "You probably know all this stuff already," I said. "It's real easy to cut down on bringing lots of clothes just by learning to mix and match."

Paula nodded, smiling at her twin. "Kayla does that sort of thing automatically, don't you?"

Kayla brightened, glancing down at her matching yellow camp shirt and tennies. "I don't mean to boast, but it does seem to come quite naturally for me."

On that note, Andie inched down in her seat, pulling her legs under her. "I'm gonna snooze for a couple hours now, if you don't mind."

Snoozing sounded like the perfect solution to getting up much too early, along with being a good way to survive the long ride ahead of us. Except for one thing. I loved the mountains, and for me, experiencing a glorious sunrise while touring the Rockies was a fabulous way to begin a week of church camp. While my friends slept, I savored a pink and purple celebration of sunlight, a kaleidoscope of my favorite colors!

At that moment, I had a strong desire to record my feelings. I missed my journal already. Staring lazily out the window, I let my thoughts go. Let my body relax, too. The tensions of the week—convincing Andie to help with the baking project, organizing the fund-raiser, and surviving my fainting spell—crowded my senses. I escaped by imagining that I was sitting on my window seat back home.

I had always loved the way the sunlight filtered into my room above my cozy spot. Sometimes the light sprang in like a rowdy spotlight; other times like a warm, sleepy hello. The padded seat itself was surrounded by a window, longer than it was tall. And because Daddy built the house back before I was born, I always figured he'd had some secret insight into my future snugglings there.

My window seat stood for many things, but the most important were privacy and the feeling of security I had when I sat there journal in hand, with Goofey, my cat, purring nearby. Just a few of the amenities writing freaks like me had to sacrifice in order to go to camp. It would be 168 long hours before I could register my thoughts about life. And God.

❤   ❤   ❤

After stops for refueling and rest rooms, we arrived on the outskirts of Ouray, a picturesque relic of old mining days. Surrounded by towering rock cliffs, some pinnacles as high as 5,000 feet, the place was hopping with tourists.

Among other things, Ouray offered all-day jeep trips and a hot springs pool which the Ute Indians had called sacred long ago. It also had high mountain meadows and herds of wildlife, not to mention Box Canyon with its 500-foot walk to a thundering waterfall.

Outdoor adventure, here we come!

The bus wound its way through an alpine meadow via a dirt road dotted with zillions of wildflowers—blazing orange Indian paintbrushes and blue and white Colorado columbines.

When we came to a clearing, the bus jolted to a stop. Instantly, sleepers awakened, yawning and stretching. I leaped out of my seat and over Andie, drowsy from her nap, and picked my way through the maze of passengers. I was the first one off the bus. Outside, I breathed in the clean, pine-scented air. Even in June, the mountain air was crisp. Perfect weather, warm and breezy. And skies bluer than blue. Birds sang their welcome—a chorus of them. I felt the warm sun on my back, and closed my eyes for a moment, realizing how very tired I was.

Behind me, I heard a twig snap. I turned around to see Pastor Rob stretching his arms and legs. He walked up the slope toward me, gazing in all directions at the rustic campsite, nestled in a secluded pine forest. "Sure beats the city any day!" he said.

"I say we're in God's country," I agreed.

"Yeah, and now it's our country—for seven days!" He clapped his hands. I turned and headed back down toward the bus, waiting for my friends.

The luggage war had begun, and I didn't have the energy to fight it. I wished now that I'd slept on the bus. When I looked at my watch, I discovered it was only nine-forty. Seemed like forever since I'd crawled out of bed to shower and throw last-minute things into my suitcase.

Kids began spilling out of the bus. I spotted Andie and Kayla, and they motioned to me, whispering to each other. Suddenly, Stan was right there talking to them. Danny, too.

I rushed to Andie's side just as I heard her ask him—no, tell him—to please disappear.

Bravo!

And Kayla, well, I could see by the frown on her pretty face, Danny Myers was definitely history. Only thing was, it hadn't quite registered with him. Maybe because she was being so cordial to him— due to the fact that Pastor Rob was close enough to touch.

But soon Rob got involved in helping kids find

their bags, and it was just us. That's when Kayla got up her nerve and told Danny to hit the road. "It's over," she said. Quietly, yet firmly.

Danny wasn't giving up. "If something's wrong, Kayla, I'm sure we can work it out," he implored.

Andie stepped forward. "There's plenty wrong, preacher-man." She pointed at him, thumping the air with her finger.

"Yo, Danny!" Billy yelled for help with a pile of luggage.

"Coming!" Danny called back. But before he left he looked at Kayla and started to apologize. "Look, I'm real sorry about whatever it was that—"

"We're wrong for each other," she interrupted.

Danny shook his head and looked at me. "Holly, can we talk later?"

"Me?" I squeaked, feeling extremely awkward about being stuck in the middle.

Andie grabbed my arm. Kayla's, too. "C'mon, girls, let's not over-exert ourselves." Danny's eyebrows shot up as she pulled us away.

Pastor Rob whistled for silence and began to distribute maps of the campground as well as the schedule for the week. We stood around in clusters, trying to pay attention to his instructions. It wasn't easy, though. Danny and Billy kept looking over at Kayla and Paula. Stan, on the other hand, completely ignored Andie. And me.

As was previously planned, Pastor Rob assigned Amy-Liz to Cabin B, already packed to capacity. "Hey, which of you girls is going to sleep on the floor?" Pastor Rob joked, eyeballing Andie and me.

"I will," I said, not certain how hard the floor of a log cabin might be.

"Let's locate an extra sleeping bag for Holly," Rob said. "She'll need it for the padding." He signaled for Jared to check for an extra one.

Jared ran down the hill to the bus. He poked his head into the luggage chamber and was still rummaging around searching for the elusive sleeping bag when I caught up with him.

"I'll do it," I said. No way was I going to let a guy help me with something so simple.

"It's no trouble, Holly-Heart." He flashed his most flirtatious grin.

"No, I mean it, Jared. Let me do it!"

He threw up his hands and stepped back. "Fine, have it your way." And he left without another word.

Andie showed up, looking for her stuff. Paula and Kayla had very little trouble spotting their things. Their luggage looked like something fresh out of a department store catalogue.

"Hey, this is camp, not Paris," Andie said, laughing at the elegant tan suitcases and the accessories to match. Just then another church bus pulled into the parking area.

"That's probably the group from Buena Vista," I said. "Isn't our counselor supposed to be on that bus?"

"What's her name again?" Andie asked.

"Rhonna Chen."

"Just pray that she's not some mopey, stringy-haired biddy," Andie teased.

"Andie Martinez!" I scolded.

Paula and Kayla blinked their eyes in synchronized rhythm. I guess that's what happens with identical twins—even if you don't have the same interests, your eyelashes can still blink to the same beat.

I couldn't help noticing some exceptionally cute guys coming off the Buena Vista bus. "C'mon, Andie," I said, leaning over and pulling her out of the luggage compartment. "We can do this later."

She didn't notice a boy wearing black cowboy jeans and boots, with hair the exact same color as mine. But I did! His T-shirt had the words "Rugged West" printed across it, and he was carrying a guitar case.

Pastor Rob whistled for us to gather around for bunk assignments. We hurried back up the hill to join the group.

After orientation, Pastor Rob introduced a lineup of all the camp counselors and staff. Mr. Boyce, the camp director, was first, followed by the cooks, custodian, and lifeguard. There were two older men, one of them bald, assigned to two of the boys' cabins. I held my breath when I spotted the women counselors. Some of them looked as old as our mothers! But none of them looked Oriental.

Where was Rhonna Chen?

Pastor Rob called out, "Cabin B." And for a split second I had visions of the week turning out to be a total bomb. Maybe we'd get a super-strict mother type and never get to have a bit of fun. Shoot, for this I could've stayed home. At least, I'd still be keeping my journal going.

Then . . . a Korean girl stepped out of the crowd.

She had delicate features and a sparkling smile. Her Mickey Mouse T-shirt and red camp shorts were perfect. She even wore a red newsboy hat atop her shoulder-length black hair.

I wanted to dance. Andie did . . . sorta.

Rhonna Chen was not only cool, she was young. And not a day over twenty!

"Man, did we luck out, or what?" Andie said later as we lugged our things up the pine-covered slope to our cabin. Counselors and kids seemed to be running everywhere with their camp gear and luggage.

"Think she's gonna be strict?" Amy-Liz asked, stopping for a breath.

"Nah." Andie shook her head. "You can tell by looking at her."

Pine needles crunched under our feet as we took the dirt path, an uphill slope all the way. We followed the path across a log bridge which arched over a rippling stream, and then a few more yards to Cabin B—our home for the week.

All of us were a little out of breath when we arrived. I held the door open to the log cabin.

Amy-Liz trailed behind with Joy and Shauna. "Are you sure you wanna sleep on the floor, Holly?" Amy-Liz asked as she dragged her bags up the wooden steps. "After all, I was the last to sign up."

"No problem," I said. "It's important for all of us to be together in one cabin."

"Maybe we can trade off," Shauna volunteered.

"Good idea," Amy-Liz said.

"Count me out," Kayla said, glancing around the room. "I have trouble sleeping on a bed, let alone on a hard floor." Paula nodded to verify her twin's remark as Kayla darted to claim the only bottom bunk left.

From the doorway, I could see our counselor crossing the narrow log bridge. She bounced as she walked, swinging her arms, yet there was a pained expression in her eyes. I stepped away from the door as she approached.

"Good morning, girls." She took off her red cap and spun it on her finger. We said good morning back.

Rhonna's face broke into a beaming smile as she leaned against the log doorjamb. Quickly, she scanned a list of names on her clipboard. Then looking up, her dark eyes studied the three sets of bunk beds. "Looks like there aren't enough beds to go around." There was a question mark in her voice.

"It'll be okay," I spoke up. "Several of us are going to trade off sleeping on the floor." Shauna and Andie nodded.

I had to make sure I thought through what I said next. No way did I want to let on what Andie and I had done to get our friend here. I explained, "Amy-Liz just found out she could come, and we wanted her to be with us in Cabin B."

The girls cheered. Hilariously.

Rhonna held up her hand, grinning. "Okay, okay," she said, trying to quiet us down. "I get the picture."

She motioned for us to sit down. Joy climbed up with Shauna on one of the top bunks. Andie and I sat on the floor near Paula and Kayla, who sat side by side on Kayla's lower bunk.

Rhonna glanced around the room at each of us. "We have seven days to get acquainted with each other, but if you've been to camp before, you know how fast the days zip by."

We nodded in unison as she filled out the cabin roster.

"Well," she said, looking up, "let's not waste a single minute. Let's find out who's who."

It took us more than a half hour to go around the room telling our names, ages, favorite hobbies, and why we'd come to camp this summer. I knew almost everything about my friends, but I listened with interest when Rhonna told us about herself.

"This is my first summer as a full-fledged camp counselor." I couldn't believe she'd admit something like that. She was inviting all sorts of trouble—at least with any other bunch of girls. Us? We were six little angels!

Rhonna continued, "Last year I was a junior counselor in Grand Junction. I've always wanted to work with kids." Here she glanced at us. "I guess I should say *teens*."

We laughed.

"Well, we're in this thing together," she said, emphasizing *together*. "And I'll be as easy to get along with as I can, but I won't stand for pushing the rules. If there's one thing I have a problem with, it's rule-breakers. And bad attitudes." Her face took on a serious look. Not stern. Just serious ... like she wasn't kidding.

"My college degree will be in political science when I graduate next year, but I'm leaning toward working with young people. So—impress me, okay?"

Rhonna was charming. Not a pushover, but a fun-loving person who would probably bend over backward to get along with us this week. But there was something about her. I felt drawn to her. Why?

When Rhonna led in prayer, I felt very close to God. Almost as close as if I were at home, sitting on my window seat, having a private conversation with him. "Dear Lord," she began. "Guide us with your hand. Keep us safe . . . and in the warmth of your love. Thanks for bringing all of us together in this fantastic place—in the middle of the tallest mountains around. Let us feel the majesty of your creation, and the gentleness of your love. In Christ's name, Amen."

After prayer, we had some free time to unpack and clean up for lunch. I couldn't help sneaking looks at Amy-Liz as she unfolded her clothes and made her bed—the bunk above Andie's. She giggled with Shauna and Joy as they unpacked. Seeing her here, and happy, made up for the sunburn and the near-heatstroke I'd suffered.

Even though I was dragging from lack of sleep, inside I felt absolutely fabulous!

"Check this out," Andie said, showing off the iron-on name tags everywhere. Her mom had made her put them on everything—underwear, towels, even her socks!

"Did you carve your name in your soap?" I teased.

"Yeah, right." She threw her pillow at me, which

launched the first of many pillow fights. One of the true glories of summer camp.

Rhonna pitched in and helped make beds and get our linens and things in order. It was like she was really one of us. Why had I wondered about who we'd get for our counselor? Shoot, at this moment, in spite of a thick layer of pillow feathers stuck on my head, things couldn't have been more perfect.

NINE

Lunch was sloppy joes, potato salad, fruit cup, and chocolate chip cookies. We met in the long, rectangular-shaped log cabin which served as both a dining hall and a chapel area, as well as classrooms for several of our daily sessions throughout the week.

At one end of the hall, a white banner with the words CAMP OURAY ... HIP, HIP, HOO-RAY! hung over a massive fireplace.

Even without air-conditioning, the all-purpose area was comfortable, probably due to plenty of open windows, allowing the mountain air to circulate. Outside temperatures were typically in the low eighties this time of year, but the near zero percent humidity played a big factor in maintaining the comfort index.

And no mosquitoes! Not even a common housefly survived in such high altitudes. No wonder tourists flocked to Ouray in the summer.

At the opposite end of the dining area, the kitchen

and serving line were well laid out and quite suitable for a room this size. Andie and I, along with our friends, quickly found a table together.

Amy-Liz started telling about last Tuesday when Pastor Rob had called with the news about the camp scholarship. "I just couldn't believe it," she exclaimed, her face shining with happiness.

We shared her excitement, but no one uttered a word about the zillions of cookies we'd made and sold to make her camp dream come true.

Halfway through the meal, Jared came over and started talking and flirting with Amy-Liz. Since he and I were ancient history, it was no big deal.

What was a big deal came shortly after. While I was ignoring Jared, paying more attention to my plate of food than to him, he grabbed my braid. And just like that, he slid the hair band off the end of it.

I spun around. "Hey! Give it back!"

But Jared was already out of reach, dodging two guys carrying lunch trays.

"Jared!" I shouted as my braid came undone. As thick as my hair was, no way would it stay braided through lunch. Not without the pink hair band. Luckily, I'd packed extras.

"Oh, Holly, your braid," Paula said sympathetically. Then turning around, she glared in Jared's direction.

I squinted my eyes like Mom does. "Why'd he do a dumb thing like that?"

"Only one reason." Andie straightened up to her full height. "He wants your attention. He hates it when females ignore him—girlfriends or not."

"Yeah, we know how he operates," Amy-Liz piped up.

"And to think I'd believed he'd changed." I thought back to the way things turned out between us at the end of eighth grade. Jared had actually seemed more settled. More mature.

Guess I was wrong.

"Once again, Wilkins snookered us." Andie rolled her eyes in disgust. "This is so-o grade school!" she observed.

"Well ... immature or not, he's got no right." I slid out from behind the bench as my hair continued to unwind.

Andie stood up, too. "I'm coming with you, Holly-Heart."

"Me too," Amy-Liz said.

Kayla wiped her lips delicately with the napkin before getting up. "Count me in."

"Make that two of us," Paula said, raising her hand like she was in school or something.

We abandoned our lunches in order to catch the culprit. "Where'd he go?" I stood in the midst of kids chowing down all around me.

"Wait a minute. There he is!" Andie pointed toward the kitchen, and we hurried to nab him.

But Jared had spotted us. He pushed open the swinging doors leading into the camp kitchen, bumping into a lady with a large basket heaped with sloppy joe buns. Up ... and out of the basket they flew. Buns everywhere.

"Hurry, let's help her," Amy-Liz said, and all seven of us raced to assist the bewildered cook.

I glared at Jared, who was acting disgustingly innocent. "Don't ever touch me again!" I shouted at him while scrambling around on the floor gathering up sloppy joe buns.

"Sorry," Jared managed to mumble amidst the chaos.

I leaped up. "No, you're not!"

Unexpectedly, he showed me both of his hands, palms open. Empty!

"Where's my hair band?" I demanded.

Jared began pulling the lining out of his pockets.

"Give it back!"

Jared turned tail and ran. "Later," he called.

"Why you!" I shouted, but by then the camp director had come to see what the commotion was about.

"Holly? Is everything all right?" Mr. Boyce asked.

I didn't know what to say. If I tattled on Jared, he'd have it in for me for the rest of the week. If I didn't tell on him, I'd probably never see my hair band again.

"I can handle it," I said, playing down the incident. Lucky for Jared.

Mr. Boyce looked at his watch. "You girls don't have much longer for lunch."

"C'mon," I said to Andie and the rest of the girls. "We better finish eating."

"I'm starved," Joy said.

"Me too," Andie said.

We hurried down the narrow aisle between the rows of foldaway tables. I wound my hair around in a makeshift bun as we headed back to our table. Then I snatched a clean fork out of the utensil tray and stuck the long end into my hair, securing the thick wad of hair.

Wouldn't you know it, that's precisely when the Buena Vista cowboy caught my eye. Feeling suddenly shy, I smiled and rolled my eyes to show that this fork-thing wasn't usual with me. His face lit up in return, surprising me.

I quickened my pace and caught up with the others. While I ate the rest of my lunch, my cabin mates shared again their woes of past male associations.

"I've had it to here with Stan," Andie spouted off, touching her eyebrows. "He's a living, walking, breathing nightmare!"

Kayla spoke right up about how horrible she thought Danny Myers had been treating her. And Paula could hardly wait to launch off on Billy Hill.

I thought we'd taken this guy thing as far into the ground as possible when Amy-Liz pushed her plate aside. "I can't believe this is happening to the rest of you! I mean, I thought I was the only one suffering from male burn-out." She muttered something about being sick of that flirt, Jared Wilkins.

Not surprised, I asked, "Is Jared bugging you now?"

"He's been calling nearly every day, talking sweet and all . . . then Shauna and I wised up and started comparing notes." Here she glanced down the table at Shauna, who nodded coyly. "We found out he's calling her after he says good-bye to me!"

"That's true," Shauna said. "Jared's doing what he does best—playing one girl against another." She looked sympathetically at Amy-Liz. "The thing is, he doesn't think he'll get caught!"

"Well, he's got another think coming!" Andie said.

Andie's cool comeback got the giggles started at our table. But across the dining hall, Stan was heading toward us, wearing a determined look.

Andie spotted him too. "Oh, this is great," she muttered. "What's he want?"

I glanced up as Stan approached our table.

"Hey, Andie," he said. "Thought I'd pick up that magazine you borrowed."

Andie shrugged like she couldn't care less.

Stan kept looking at her like the magazine was real important. "It's the one with the article on John Wayne," he explained.

"I know which one it is, and I didn't borrow it; you gave it to me," she said.

"Well, I want it back."

"Fine," Andie snapped. "It's over there with my music folder." She pointed to a row of shelves near the entrance. And without another word, Stan left.

"If you wanna know the truth, I never really liked John Wayne," Andie whispered.

"Too bad Stan's obsession with his movie hero hasn't rubbed off," I said, laughing.

Andie snickered, too. "Yeah, John Wayne could teach Stan Patterson a thing or two about women."

Kayla held her fork in midair. "Our church guys treat us essentially with no respect."

"Who needs guys anyway!" I announced, forgetting about the blond cowboy four tables away.

"I'll say amen to that," Kayla blurted out.

"Not a-men," Andie giggled. "Not *any*-men."

And once again, we totally lost it.

♥ ♥ ♥

When all of us finished eating, we waited at the door while Andie went to get her music folder. I happened to glance over where she was standing. By the frustrated look on her face I figured there was a problem. I told the others I'd be right back. Rushing to Andie's side, I discovered her plight.

"I'm gonna be in such big trouble for this." She gestured wildly. "My piano music for choir practice is gone!"

I looked around. "Where could it be?"

"I put it right here before lunch," she said, pointing to the lower shelf next to the window. "Mr. Keller won't be happy about this." She looked at her watch. "And choir's in two hours!"

I felt her rage. Probably because Andie and I had been best friends since forever. The way I figured, she had a right to be angry. After all Andie shouldered the sole responsibility of accompanying our camp choir. And she was good . . . the best around.

Today was our first scheduled rehearsal. Mr. Keller, the youth choir director from our church, expected promptness and perfection. Nothing less.

"Do you think Stan took it?" I asked, remembering the thing with his movie magazine.

Andie's countenance changed from frustration to pure anger. "That rat!"

I groaned. "Why did God have to give me such a louse for a brousin?"

Andie frowned. "What's brousin mean again?"

"It's the combination of cousin and stepbrother—"

"Never mind!" Andie was freaking out. "What's Stan want with my music anyway?"

"He's probably ticked because you dumped him."

Her face turned a rare shade of bright purple. "Well ... serves him right."

To top things off, Danny flagged us down as we were about to leave the dining hall. "Holly! Andie!" he called.

"Make it quick," Andie said.

"I saw what happened with your music," Danny said.

"We know—we know. Stan took it," Andie said sarcastically.

Danny's auburn hair was combed back neatly as usual, and he wore one of his button-down Sunday shirts, looking like he was ready to claim the nearest pulpit.

"Calm down, girls. 'A gentle answer turns away wrath, but a harsh word stirs up anger,'" he said.

"Save your breath, Danny," I replied. "It's too late for soft answers or whatever. Stan's a toad." I almost added, "and so are you," but bit my tongue.

Once again, Danny had found one of the many Proverbs stored in his vast memory bank and used it against us. Some friend!

Without looking back, Andie and I joined the girls from Cabin B, leaving Danny in the dust.

TEN

Andie told the girls about Stan and her missing music on the walk to our cabin. "I've got to have it back before choir," she said.

"Well, it's quiet time now," Paula commented. "Stan's probably off trying to be quiet somewhere like a good boy."

I smiled at her insightful remark. Coming from Paula's lips the comment was hilarious.

"Well, it won't be quiet for long when I get a hold of him!" Andie exclaimed.

Shauna had an idea. "Maybe if you're lucky, he'll bring the music along to choir."

"That won't happen," I said. "Not unless Andie begs him first."

Andie fussed. "Well, I'll just have to go track him down."

"I'll go with you," I offered. So did the rest of our cabin mates.

A sudden breeze came up, making the aspen

leaves rattle. I noticed that the sky had darkened; clouds were rolling in from the south. A summer storm was on its way.

Reaching back, I pulled the fork out of my bun and retwisted my hair into an even tighter knot, hoping it would stay.

"Why don't you just let your hair hang free?" Amy-Liz suggested. "It's so long and thick."

"And glamorous," Kayla added.

Andie disagreed. "What she really oughta do is trim it—about ten inches worth."

"Don't you wish," I said. Andie was always hinting at how I should lop off my locks.

"I know, I know, it's your best feature, right?" Andie said. I knew she was still fuming over Stan, so I overlooked her cutting remark. A loud clap of thunder and a burst of wind sent us scurrying up the path to the safety of our cabin.

Inside, I dug through my luggage and pulled out my cosmetic bag. Blush. Mascara. Deodorant. Toothbrush . . . I groaned as the truth set in.

"What's the matter?" Andie asked.

"I forgot to pack my hair bands!" I moaned. "Anyone have some I could borrow?"

I looked around. Everyone had that sorry-can't-help-you-look on their faces. Paula and Kayla always wore their hair down and permed. Andie's hair was too short for hair bands. And Shauna, Joy, and Amy-Liz only used barrettes and hair combs in their shoulder-length hair. I was sunk!

"Maybe someone from another cabin might have one you could borrow," Amy-Liz suggested.

"I can't ask a complete stranger!" I said, freaking out. I couldn't believe it. At home I had zillions of hair bands—at least two for every day of the month. But in my early-morning rush, I'd forgotten to pack extras. How could I be so stupid?

Wrong, I corrected myself. How could *Jared* be so stupid.

I stood up, a frown of determination on my face. "It's time we women unite," I declared.

Kayla looked up. "How?"

We began to talk excitedly. And our first quiet time at camp turned out to be full of noise—booming thunder outside, pounding rain on the roof, and heated discussion inside. Fortunately, Rhonna Chen was occupied for the moment—in a counselor's meeting. I'm not sure what she would have thought of the conversation we had.

"We could report Stan to the camp director and get him kicked out," Shauna said. But by the looks on everyone's face, no one was in favor of that.

"Or . . . we could form a society," I suggested, lowering my voice. "A secret society." I motioned for the girls to gather round. "We could make a pact—a 'no-guys' pact. It'll be fabulous."

"Yeah," Paula said softly. "For women only."

"Tell us more," Amy-Liz said, playing with the tops of her neon-green socks.

I nodded. "Here's the deal: We write a pact with rules and stuff. And the first big rule will be 'ignore boys.'"

Andie cheered. "Count me in!"

"You're amazing, Holly!" Amy-Liz shouted. "What'll we call our secret society?"

"How about . . ." I thought for a second, then began laughing nearly uncontrollably.

"What is it?" Andie grabbed my arm.

I couldn't stop.

"What's so funny?" Joy asked.

I coughed and sputtered, choking down the giggles. "It's perfect. Are you ready for this?"

My cabin mates leaned in even closer.

"Since the guys need a little help from their friends," I began, "we'll call it S.O.S., which stands for 'Sisters of Silence.' Get it—S.O.S.? Help for the guys—to teach them how to treat women."

The girls applauded.

"You and your wild abbreviations," Andie said.

"Remember that scrutiny test she put Jared through last fall?" Kayla asked. "What was it called again?"

"S-T-A-N," Andie recited.

"Thanks," I said, tickled that they'd remembered. "So . . . what do you think about S.O.S.?"

"Well, I'll be delighted to join," said Kayla. "Show me where to sign."

"I'll show you, all right," I said, pulling my suitcase out from under Andie's bed. Thank goodness I'd packed my new spiral notebook!

I sat on the floor, using the top of Andie's suitcase as a desk. With pen in hand, on lined paper, I wrote down our pact. The girls sat on the floor peering over my shoulder, some of them whispering to themselves as they read each sentence. Bottom line: We would ignore all boys to the best of our ability for the rest of camp week. Here's what we wrote:

The "No-Guys" Pact

We, the Sisters of Silence, on this twenty-third day of June, do promise and resolve to ignore the boys at Ouray Camp for the space of one week.

We may speak quickly, such as "Hi," or respond to a boy's greeting, but we will not be involved in any extended conversation.

We will not accept dates in a group or alone.

We will not sit with a boy in chapel.

We will not eat any meals with a boy.

We will not sit around the campfire with a boy.

By following the above provisions, we hope to help the male population of this camp learn to respect us.

Everyone cheered when I wrote the final word. Andie was the first to sign her name. She handed the pen back to me, and I signed next. Then came Paula, Kayla, Amy-Liz, Shauna, and Joy.

We sealed the pact with bright pink nail polish, the Miller twins' expensive stuff. When the polish dried a bit, I pressed my pen into the gooey substance and printed the letters S.O.S.

There. Now our pact was signed and sealed.

This was just the beginning!

ELEVEN

Paula broke the solemn silence. "When does the pact legally begin?" She fluffed her bangs for no obvious reason.

"Immediately!" Amy-Liz replied.

"Hurray!" shouted the Sisters of Silence.

It was time for celebration all right, and if I were at home, I'd be reaching for my journal right now. I went to the cabin window and stood by it staring out just as I did every day on my window seat at home. The rain had slowed up, and the sun had created a golden ribbon around the thunderclouds above.

Andie came up to me. "What's up?"

"Oh, just thinking about that rotten Jared person we used to fight over. Remember?" I turned to face her.

"The first love of your life is a thief, Holly," she said softly. Sadly.

I nodded. "I want my hair band back so bad I can taste it!"

Andie stopped nibbling on her candy bar and offered it to me. "Here, try this."

I laughed. So did Amy-Liz, who'd overheard us talking. But the missing piano scores were no laughing matter. Andie *had* to find her music before choir.

It was already one-thirty. Time for craft class for some of us. Archery for the rest.

"Let's go," I said. "Rhonna shouldn't be coming back here before we do. You know how long-winded those counselors can get in their meetings."

Kayla suggested pushing a chair under the doorknob so no one could rip off our stuff while we were gone. "But, wait, how will we get out of here?" she asked.

Andie spied the back window and went to check out the situation. "Looks like this one's close enough to the ground," she said. "We can jump out over here."

And that's what we did. We stuffed a chair under the doorknob and left through the back window.

Just as I was swinging my left leg over the window sill, I heard someone jiggle the doorknob. I froze. Sat right there on the ledge like a shot pigeon.

"C'mon, Holly," Paula said from outside, reaching up to assist me. "Are you afraid to jump?"

"It's not that," I said, lowering my voice. "Someone's at our front door!"

I heard knocking. "Anyone home?" a voice called.

I whispered out the window to the girls, "It's Rhonna!"

The Silent Sisters freaked out.

"Quick! Everyone back inside!" Then to Rhonna I called, "Uh, just a minute. I'll be right there."

It was the only logical solution. If we were caught leaving through the window and barring the door like this, well, I wasn't sure what might follow.

My heart pounded as Andie and Shauna pulled Joy back through the window and into the cabin.

"Not a word about anything," I whispered, before removing the chair from under the doorknob.

Rhonna came inside, smiling. I'd expected a tongue-lashing for blocking the door like that. But she was as cool as you can get—still wearing her red cap. Only now it sat sideways on her jet-black hair. "Having a private meeting, girls?"

We nodded, grinning like crazy, and not because we were happy. Because we were so lucky.

She glanced at her watch. "So, who's doing crafts today?" she asked, looking around.

Andie, Paula, and I raised our hands.

"Anyone for archery?"

That took care of Kayla, Amy-Liz, Shauna, and Joy.

"Okay, let's go," Rhonna said, still smiling. It was like she remembered how it was being a teen at camp. Without another word, we split up and headed in different directions.

During basket weaving class, my hair came loose three times. I had to keep winding it into a bun because it was too thick and heavy to stay put. Mrs. Campbell, the expert basket weaver and instructor, finally gave me a long pencil to stick in it. The pencil worked much better. Probably looked better, too.

More important than my hair, though, was Andie's

music. She was worried sick. And I *had* to do something. After all, Stan was my brousin. If I couldn't outsmart him, no one could.

Finally I excused myself, using the rest room as my reason to leave.

I left the great hall via the same exit as Stan had at lunch almost two hours ago. Which way had he gone? I wondered, following the dirt path to the front of the building.

I needed something to go on. Just one minuscule shred of evidence . . .

Hiding behind the trunk of a dripping wet poplar tree, I spied out the land. I peered down, scanning the path carefully and the wild grass on either side of it, hoping to find a clue.

To my far right were the guys' cabins; to my left, the girls'. In front of me, the commons area stretched across a flat, wide meadow bordered by tall pine trees that rose like pointed arrows straight to the sky. A flagpole stood in the center of the area. Behind that lay the sports area and pool.

I decided to scout things out in Stan's cabin. Surely, that's where he'd hidden the music folder. But I'd have to go around to the back of the great hall so I wouldn't be seen by the kids in the craft class. Mrs. Campbell would know I hadn't gone to the rest room if she spied me sneaking across the commons area to the boys' side of the camp.

I backtracked, heading around the back of the dining hall. Down the steep slope behind it was the amphitheater, and even farther down, a rugged, wild area of rocks and cliffs leading to the valley floor. I sneaked down low, so I wouldn't be seen by the cooks in the back windows.

Crouching down, I noticed the blond cowboy carrying his raincoat and hurrying to the boys' cabin. Curious, I followed close behind.

He went inside the cabin. Probably to drop off his raincoat, I thought. One look at the sky and I knew the shower had passed. I stood outside the cabin, wondering what to do now that I was here. I certainly couldn't barge right in with him inside!

That's when he came out, looking mighty surprised to see me. Surprised ... and definitely pleased.

"Hi," I managed to say.

His eyes searched mine.

"Have you seen a music folder with Andie Martinez written on the top?" I described the size and color.

"Oh, that." He disappeared into the cabin and emerged carrying the folder under his arm. "Stan Patterson found this somewhere," he said.

"No, he didn't find it," I insisted. "Stan stole it!"

He frowned. "Are you sure?"

"Positive. Danny Myers saw everything," I said, referring to the moment in the dining hall. "Stan's mad at Andie. That's why he did this."

His face lit up, bright with amusement. "Looks like you're mad, too." Suddenly, I remembered the pact. *No extended conversation.*

"Uh, thanks for this," I said, turning to leave. "You saved Andie's life!"

But he called after me. "Wait!"

I turned around.

"I hope I'll see you again, Holly."

He knew my name!

The afternoon sun enhanced the blondness of his hair. And the blue in his T-shirt brought out the blue in his eyes. "My name's Todd. Todd Stillson." He paused. "What're you doin' later?" he asked. "Maybe we could take a walk ... or something."

We will not accept single or group dates with a guy.

"Look, I'm sorry ... I've gotta go." I forced my gaze away from his face and started down the path toward the dining hall, proud that I'd stuck to the rules of our S.O.S. pact.

"Holly?" he called after me.

I kept walking. Proudly walking away.

TWELVE

Andie leaped out of her chair when I returned with her music folder. She hugged me. And . . . *whoosh!* My hair came tumbling down. Again.

"Oops, sorry," she said, giggling.

"No problem." I redid my bun.

Andie held the music folder close. "Where'd you find this?" she whispered.

"It's a long story."

Mrs. Campbell glanced up, nodding. "Everything okay?" she asked, coming over to our table. I had been gone quite a while.

"I'm fine, thanks."

She scrutinized my half-woven basket, then looked at me a little too sympathetically. "If you hurry, hon, I think you can finish your project today."

"I'll try," I said, smiling. The smile was really for Andie and for having retrieved her music. A triumph!

When the teacher left to help someone else, Andie whispered in my ear, "Tell me." I should've known she wouldn't give up easily.

"Todd Stillson found it in his cabin," I said, enjoying the sound of Todd's name on my lips.

After crafts class, we waited for Mr. Keller to arrive for choir. Jared, Danny, Stan, and a bunch of kids from Buena Vista started showing up. Todd came, too.

All of us in Cabin B sat on one side of the stage area, which also doubled as the platform for chapel services. We women were sticking together, all right. Making a statement about not needing men.

My hair kept coming loose, and it was really starting to bug me. And how awful that it had to happen in front of Todd!

Andie offered an idea. "As a favor from one friend to another, I'm gonna chop your hair off tonight . . . while you're asleep."

"You wouldn't!"

"Maybe, maybe not," she teased.

Acquiring something as ordinary as a music folder had completely rejuvenated my friend. As for my stolen hair band, well, I didn't dare think about it, or I'd come uncorked.

The side door opened, and Mr. Keller burst into the room. He motioned for Andie to move to the piano. I watched her take her seat and arrange her music. I was certain that she'd never follow through with her threat. Besides, she was a heavy sleeper.

Reaching up, I touched my hair. Maybe I could braid it later, do something to make the ends hard, to keep it from unraveling. Elmer's glue might be a possibility, I thought. Glue washes out.

Mr. Boyce showed up, and while he spoke with Mr. Keller about our Sunday chapel performance, I wondered if he might have some extra rubber bands floating around in his office. Surely he wouldn't mind offering assistance to a damsel in distress. The more I thought about it, the more I knew it was something worth pursuing. I would pay the camp director an impromptu visit right after choir.

Mr. Keller and Mr. Boyce stepped outside, and Jared took advantage of the moment. "Ps-st, Holly!"

I turned around without thinking.

A pink flash!

Jared waved my hair band in midair. Then, in a split second, it disappeared back into his pocket.

"What a child," Paula said.

"We really shouldn't have looked at him," I whispered to her.

"In keeping with the pact we made, you're right," Paula said. "*Ignore* is the key word."

By now Kayla and Amy-Liz were leaning forward in their seats, trying to hear what Paula and I were saying.

"We'll discuss this later," I assured them. The six of us—Andie was sitting prim and proper at the piano—leaned back in our chairs. Almost on cue. That synchronized motion surely had Jared and Danny wondering by now. In fact, the guys were beginning to lose it. Todd, however, looked more confused than amused.

Jared whispered that my hair looked like something out of *Little Women*.

I didn't flinch or move a muscle. A little respect would've been in order about now. After all, we were

103

in the area where chapel services were held. Where worship and praise was given to God.

"Hey, Holly!" Jared called to me again.

I kept ignoring him.

"We've been talking about you. And we were wondering ..." He paused dramatically to get everyone's attention. "... did you notice that a flying saucer has landed on your head—complete with antenna?" He pointed at the pencil.

There was rousing group laughter now. And out of the jeering crowd I heard, quite distinctly, my stepbrother's voice.

That Stan, I thought sadly. *He's just as rotten as the rest of them.* Humiliated, I wanted to melt into the floor. But I kept my cool and refused to look at Jared. Or at any of the rest of them. I didn't even look at Todd, who hadn't joined in the laughter at all.

Paula reached over and touched my arm. "Don't pay attention to them, Holly-Heart," she said. "Your hair's beautiful no matter how you fix it."

I smiled. Leave it to Paula to comfort me. What a good friend she'd turned out to be. I felt more confident than ever about the pact. S.O.S. was working! My sisters and I were in agreement—a unified front.

When Mr. Keller returned, he allowed us to stay seated for the first song. "It's good to see so many of you here," he said without cracking a smile. "Mr. Boyce tells me that we should have two numbers prepared for Sunday morning."

He went on to remind us not to chew gum, talk when he was talking, or sing like a soloist. "Blending is everything." He adjusted his wild purple tie. "I don't need thirty show-offs in here. If you want to make a statement, sign up for horseback riding, please." His face broke into a wide grin. "Any takers?"

No one.

The question was designed to weed out smart alecks on the first day of practice.

"Good! Now, sing as though your life depended on it," he shouted. "Because it might."

We laughed along with him. That was Mr. Keller. He spoke precisely what was on his mind. The nice thing about people like that is you always know exactly what's expected. Exactly where you stand.

As for standing, we lined up when we sight-read the second song. I stood proudly with my Sisters of Silence, ignoring Jared, Danny, and Stan. Billy Hill was missing. Evidently, he was out riding a horse ... making a statement.

After choir, we had fifteen minutes before afternoon devotions. My sisters were headed off to the rest rooms when I explained that I was going to hunt down some rubber bands.

Mr. Boyce's office was housed in a former boys' cabin. The exterior was even more rustic than the other cabins, and I noticed several chairs lined up on the porch. Apparently the counselors had gathered there for their meeting.

I felt strange marching off in the direction of the camp director's cabin. Jared seemed uneasy, too, when I passed him standing near the flagpole. I made a point to walk with determination—straight for Mr. Boyce's office.

"Holly!" Jared said as though nothing had happened earlier. "Let's talk!"

Oh, yeah, Wilkins. Not on your life.

Suddenly, it dawned on me why Jared might be so concerned. Maybe he thought I was going to report him for taking my hair band. Perfect!

"Holly!" Jared called again. "Wait up!"

I chuckled to myself. Jared was playing right into my hands.

He caught up with me. "Where're you going?"

I spun around. "Where do you *think* I'm going?"

"Hey, relax," he said, taking a step backward. "This is camp, remember?"

"I remember, all right," I said. "Now, if you'll excuse me, I have to see Mr. Boyce."

He threw an anxious glance at the camp director's office just ahead. "C'mon, Holly, lighten up."

"Later." I pushed past him.

"Wait, you're not gonna—"

"Not gonna what?"

"Listen, Holly, will you drop this if I give your hair band back?"

Bingo!

I turned around, holding out my hand silently. Jared reached into his pocket and pulled out my pink hair band.

Looking around, I hoped my sisters weren't watching. *Extended conversation.* Indeed! The words pounded my brain.

Here I was less than two hours into the pact, and I had already broken the first rule.

THIRTEEN

"Happy now?" Jared asked.

I ignored him, trying to make up for the pact rule I'd already fractured.

He cleared his throat. "Uh, Holly, could I ask you a favor?"

"Nope."

"C'mon. We're still friends, aren't we?"

"That depends."

"Look, I think you could be a little, uh . . ."

"What?" I snapped.

"A little friendlier," came the reply.

"Forget it!"

"Why?" he asked. "What's going on?"

"None of your business." I turned, clutching my hair band, and ran across the grassy area toward the path leading to the girls' rest room. At last, I could get rid of this crazy bun!

I heard a group of kids laughing and talking as they came up the slope from horseback riding class.

Several girls from Buena Vista were with them, along with Billy Hill.

I darted inside the bathrooms, yanking the pencil out of my mound of hair. Like a waterfall, my hair cascaded around me. So much for bunhead!

Luckily, my cabin mates were still there. They'd finished washing up, and now they were primping in front of the mirrors.

"Look, everyone!" I waved the hair hand. "I got it back!"

They crowded around me, buzzing. "How did you do it?" Andie asked.

I peered under a few stalls. "Anyone else here?" I asked. No way did I want outsiders overhearing what I was about to say!

"Just us," Amy-Liz piped up.

"Good." And I told them what I'd done.

Shauna and Joy listened intently as I told my tale. Kayla and Paula stopped combing their hair and stood, spellbound, brushes in hand. Andie looked on with ever-widening eyes.

"But—" I concluded, making a face. "I feel bad that I had to break the pact to get my hair band back. I said I wouldn't have any extended conversation with a boy, and now—"

"Well, you didn't talk to him *that* long!" Shauna interrupted.

"Besides," Amy-Liz chimed in, "you only did it to get your hair band back."

"And in a decidedly clever manner!" Paula observed.

My Sisters of Silence were so sweet and forgiving

that I began to calm down and feel better. Until Andie spoke up.

"Okay, enough sympathy," she said, clapping her hands briskly. Her dark eyes were fixed on me. "Holly broke the very first rule of our pact. It's not the end of the world, but it should never happen again!"

I looked around, hoping to get some support, but they all looked down at their shoes, refusing to meet my gaze. The Sisters of Silence were *too* silent. Here I was, supposedly on friendly—sisterly—turf, having just suffered a tremendous blow to my self-esteem, and Andie sounded like she was threatening to kick me out of my own secret society!

"I know I'll do better next time," I said. Just then Todd's smiling face flashed into my mind. Would I be able to keep from talking to him next time?

The girls' solemn faces told me I'd better—or else.

FOURTEEN

Luckily, the bell rang for devotions right then, so me and my pact-breaking were forgotten in the rush to put the last touches on makeup and hair.

Once again we all gathered in the main hall. Danny was seated behind the pulpit with Mr. Boyce and Pastor Rob. I nudged Andie, rolling my eyes. "Look who they got to preach," I joked. "Pastor Danny!"

Sure enough. After Mr. Boyce opened with prayer and Pastor Rob led us in a few songs, Danny stood up and gave a high and mighty exposition on a verse in Ephesians—about becoming mature in the faith. I hoped Jared was paying attention!

Todd was sitting two rows in front of me. His hair was charmingly messy. I could tell he wasn't a guy who was always checking himself out in a mirror. Not like Jared—Mr. Vanity himself.

Then I caught myself. *C'mon, Holly*, I scolded. *You*

need to ignore the boys—all boys. Cute and troublesome alike.

The secret society had to come first. *Besides, there's always next year*, I thought, proud that I was sticking to my resolution.

After chapel, Todd came up to me. "Hi, Holly," he said, falling in step with me.

My face grew warm.

"Last one to Cabin B's a poached egg!" Andie announced as we approached the front entrance.

Amy-Liz, Shauna, and Joy dashed off, leaving the Miller twins and me behind. They gave me a searching glance. I could tell they'd noticed Todd. Todd with me!

"Let's go!" I shouted, thankful for a graceful excuse to ignore Todd. Speeding up, I forced myself to match strides with Paula and Kayla. They had been on the track team during spring semester and were still in great shape.

The thing that slowed me down was the steep slope leading to our cabin. At last, exhausted from lack of sleep and too winded to go on, I slowed down. That's when I saw Rhonna.

She was coming out of the camp office, and her eyes were red. Had she been crying?

"Hi, Rhonna," I said.

She smiled a little. "How was devotions?" she asked. But I could tell she really didn't care.

"Are you okay?" I asked.

She nodded quickly, then shrugged her shoulders. "Well ... no, I'm not," she said. "Truth is, I was just talking to my mom. She and my dad are going through a pretty nasty divorce."

"Oh," I said. "I'm sorry."

"Your parents are divorced, right?" Rhonna asked. I had explained my weird family situation during the introduction time.

"Yeah. It was really hard at first," I said. "But that was a long time ago."

She had a faraway look in her dark eyes. "The only thing that seems to help these days is running. I get up early and jog till I drop. Every day."

I hardly knew what to say to her, even though she seemed so open and friendly—not nearly as adult and distant as I'd expected.

"Maybe your parents will work things out," I offered—the fantasy I'd entertained in my own mind—and heart—for many years.

"No hope of that, Holly," she said softly. "Unfortunately."

"I'm sorry."

She nodded, adjusting her red cap. "So am I."

That seemed to end our conversation—at least that aspect of it. Now I knew what had drawn me to her earlier. Now I understood the pain in her eyes. I determined to keep the information quiet. Just between the two of us.

When we arrived at the cabin, Kayla was applying mascara to her already dark lashes. Joy and Shauna leaned into the wall mirror like Siamese twins attached at the shoulders.

Andie was obviously ready for supper; in fact, it appeared that she couldn't wait another minute. She reached under her bunk and pulled a blueberry muffin out of a shoe box.

Not surprised, I watched her hide her stash of leftovers under her bed. "You're not hoarding food, are you?" I teased.

She didn't seem to mind. "It's just in case I get hungry in the middle of the night."

Reaching for my brush, I unbraided my hair, brushed it out, then put it in a ponytail high on my head. After wiping my face with astringent, I applied some fresh makeup. Since the cabin was a bit crowded, I went outside and sat on the porch, waiting for the rest of the girls.

Rhonna sat on the porch too, Bible in hand. I didn't know if she was preparing for our evening devotions—or finding some comfort in her situation. I let her read quietly.

I thought of the secret pact and wondered what Rhonna would think of the drastic measures my Sisters of Silence and I had taken.

The supper bell rang. Five-thirty.

Rhonna closed her Bible, then gave me a sweet "don't-worry-about-me" smile. It seemed that reading the Bible had really helped.

"Girls!" she called, clapping her hands together.

When we'd all gathered on the porch, she announced, "We're going to have fun tonight. We have plans to get all of you interacting with each other."

Andie looked at me, frowning. "Like how?"

"Oh, you'll see," Rhonna said secretively.

"Tell us!" the girls shouted, swarming around her.

Rhonna wrinkled her nose. "Among other things, you get to pick someone you don't know and spend ten minutes talking to that person."

I groaned inwardly. This could be real tricky for the S.O.S.! The rest of the girls stared wide-eyed.

"What?" Rhonna said, raising her hands. "Did I say something wrong?"

Andie rolled her eyes. "Oh, no. Nothing at all."

Rhonna looked surprised. Probably at the lack of enthusiasm from us, and the sarcastic way Andie had responded. "C'mon, girls, here's your chance to meet some new guys," she prodded, obviously thinking we'd be overjoyed at the thought.

Guys? Right.

The mere mention of the word made us sick.

FIFTEEN

At supper, we filled up one whole table. We took our time eating, chattering about the events of the first day at camp. But we avoided any mention of the pact since Rhonna was sharing the meal with us.

But we did ignore the boys. Ignored them in spite of their continuous attempts to get our attention. All through supper, Stan, Billy, Danny, and, of course, Jared kept watching us.

Once Danny strolled past our table, obviously going out of his way to get seconds. Not one of us spoke as he waved, smiled, and then . . . frowned. Andie nearly choked trying to keep a straight face.

And to make the boys even more jealous, we got into a string of joke-telling.

Andie got us started. "What did the upper denture say to the lower denture?" she asked.

Kayla bit. "What?"

"We're going out tonight," Andie said.

"O-o-oh, Andie," the girls groaned. "Sick joke."

We knew the guys wondered what on earth was so funny!

"Here's another one," Andie said, glancing over at the guys' table. "It's better."

"It *better* be," I said.

"What kind of boat does a dentist like best?"

None of us knew.

Andie grinned. "A tooth ferry!"

Then came a flood of camp riddles. Shauna got them going. Then the Miller twins each had a turn. I kept waiting for Rhonna to share a good riddle. But she was silent, observing more than I cared for her to see. "I know," Andie said again. "Here's one I just made up."

She glanced at me. "Did you know Jared spent all night trying to wake up his sleeping bag?"

We laughed, forgetting ourselves for the moment. Rhonna looked around at us, a small frown on her face. "Who's Jared?" she asked when we'd calmed down a bit.

We shot glances at each other. But no one said a word. The pact thing was top-secret. Not even a cool counselor should know about it.

When it came time to clean up tables and get ready for the orientation, I caught Todd looking at me. He was sitting between Jared and Danny, and I wondered if they'd filled him in on what a sweet person I was. Seriously, I wondered what rotten things they'd said about me. I tried to avoid looking at him.

Ignoring Todd worked well enough until Mr. Boyce asked everyone to introduce themselves. I spotted a redheaded girl with braces two tables away and hightailed it over there. My sisters hurried to make contact with several new girls from Buena Vista, as well. We were meticulous in following the rules of our pact. I was doing well, that is, until Todd intercepted me.

"Hi, again," he said.

"Oh, hi." I had no idea what to say next.

"How's your first day at camp?"

"Okay," I said, mindful of the pact.

"You doing anything special for Talent Night next Wednesday?" he asked.

Everyone loved the big finale—the last fabulous night at camp. But I hadn't even begun to think about what I'd be doing.

"Well . . . I sing," I mentioned feebly.

"Great!" he said. "I play guitar. Will you sing a duet with me?"

A duet? With Todd? I swallowed hard.

"Oh, that's very nice of you," I managed to say, "but—"

Andie waved at me. Frowning.

"Excuse me a second," I said to Todd, and rushed over to see what Andie wanted.

She was caught up in animated conversation with one of the girls. Turning to me, she said, "Holly, you remember Alissa Morgan, don't you? You took her spot during the spring choir tour in seventh grade?"

Of course I remembered. If it hadn't been for Alissa leaving Dressel Hills, I might never have gone out with Danny Myers.

Andie kept talking. "This is Alissa's cousin, Emily. She likes to write stories, too."

"Hi," I said, wondering what to do about Todd, who was still standing off to the side, probably waiting for my return.

"I read one of your stories," Emily said. "In that magazine, *Sealed With A Kiss*."

"You did?"

Emily nodded. "Your story, wasn't it called something like, 'Double Love,' or ..." She paused. "I don't remember the exact title, but it was great."

"Thanks," I said, deciding not to correct her. The actual title had been "Love Times Two."

I noticed the pin on the collar of Emily's camp shirt. It was a simple gold pen, and seeing it and meeting her made me miss my journal.

Mr. Boyce asked us to take our seats, ending the ten-minute encounter. The entire staff, including camp nurse, maintenance, and cooks had assembled and were ready to be introduced formally.

My mind, however, was on Todd, that cute cowboy who wanted *me* to sing a duet with him.

I sighed. Was it breaking the pact rules to stare at a guy?

❤   ❤   ❤

Back in the cabin, it was almost lights out.

I couldn't help myself; I opened my suitcase and located the spiral notebook containing the S.O.S. pact rules. I wasn't referring to the rules or anything. I just needed a blank page. I had to write!

Way in the back of the notebook, where no one would ever see, I began my secret camp journal.

Thursday night, June 23rd: I can't believe how

exhausted I am. We walk everywhere—to chapel, to classes, to the dining hall. Saturday, a big hike is planned. I'm worn out just thinking about it. And peeling like crazy. But, oh well, getting sunburned was worth getting Amy-Liz to camp. She's having a marvelous time.

This guy, no this wonderful person, Todd Stillson, asked me to sing a duet with him for Talent Night next week. I'm torn apart—ripped, really. If I snub Todd, he'll think I'm rude. But how can I compromise the Sisters of Silence? (That's our secret society.)

I must be true to the pact—it's a "No-Guys" pact, a list of things we absolutely refuse to do this week. The guys have it coming . . . Our Dressel Hills guys, that is.

The first day of camp has been a nightmare!

There was so much whispering going on, nobody paid any attention to my journal and me. Thank goodness! When I closed the spiral notebook, I slipped it safely into my suitcase and closed the lid.

There were three rounds of pillow fights before Rhonna signaled lights out. That's when the giggling started. And the secrets . . .

Secrets like who got their period first, and what each of us thought it would be like to be kissed. On the lips, of course. Since none of us really knew, it was up for total speculation.

Shauna said it would feel like a rubber band smooshing against her lips.

I disagreed. "I think it'll be fabulous . . . if it's true love, of course. His lips will be warm and soft, and—"

"Juicy!" Amy-Liz squealed. That got us wired up.

Amy-Liz got the bright idea to practice kissing. On our arms, not each other.

It was a good thing the cabin was dark. And Rhonna was too tired to care. Or at least she was pretending to be asleep. Her parents' divorce seemed heavy on her mind.

Andie sneezed. "This isn't working," she whispered. "My arm's too hairy to be someone's lips!"

"Pretend he's got a mustache," I said.

"Good idea," Andie said, and went back to smooching.

Eventually, all of us got tired and fell asleep.

SIXTEEN

Rhonna's alarm clock went off, shattering my early-morning dreams.

Friday. Second day at camp.

I groaned and rolled over. *Let Rhonna do her pre-dawn jogging thing*, I thought as I fell back to sleep.

Soon the rise and shine bell rang. I sat up—half of me still in my sleeping bag—and reached for my suitcase. Inside, I discovered some stationery and three self-addressed stamped envelopes.

Mom.

She knew me well. I wrote her a quick letter, assuming that Uncle Jack would read it, too. I wrote about Rhonna Chen, our cool counselor, and all the fun we were having. I left out the S.O.S. and the "No-Guys" pact, of course.

I could almost see Mom sipping iced peppermint tea on the front-porch swing of our home as she read my letter to Uncle Jack. When I licked the envelope, I sensed a twinge of homesickness. Just a twinge.

It was Joy who had a serious case, I discovered on

our way to the showers. As we headed down the dirt path and over the log bridge, she confided her feelings. Not only was she homesick, she was worried about what the camp had cooked up for breakfast.

"Let's see if we can't get you some vegetarian meals," I suggested.

Joy slipped her gym bag over her shoulder. "That's sweet of you, Holly. Thanks."

I stuck close to Joy when we went swimming later that afternoon. Homesickness is untreatable and can turn into a debilitating disease. The rest of the Silent Sisters were extra nice to her, too.

We weren't being very nice to the guys, though. In fact, the pact and all its implications were beginning to take shape. Not only were we living up to our rule of no extended conversation, we weren't even returning "hi's." "Byes" were out, too. So was everything else verbal.

We acted as though the guys weren't even sharing the same pool with us, steering clear of them so effectively that none of us noticed what was going on outside the pool. Outside . . . on the grassy area where we'd laid out our beach towels and sport bags.

Andie and I were getting out of the pool when Paula and Kayla let out matching shrieks. I turned to see what the noise was about.

"Our sport bags are gone," Paula wailed.

"With our *expensive* makeup!" Kayla cried.

"What?" I said. Andie and I dashed over to check on our belongings.

Shauna was already shouting. "Mine's gone, too!"

Sure enough, not a single one of us had a stitch of makeup. Or clothes.

Amy-Liz put her hands on her tiny hips. "You don't suppose—"

"Yes, I do!" I shouted. "I think the guys know something about this."

Kayla looked like she was going to cry. "We *have* to get our stuff back!"

"Wait, girls!" Andie called out. We stopped chattering and looked at her. "We're not going to let the boys get to us, right?"

We nodded.

"We're committed to ignoring them, right?"

We nodded again.

"It's really no big deal not having makeup, *right*?" She stared at each of us in turn. And like loyal sisters, we nodded again. In sync.

"And," she concluded, "we've got plenty of clothes back at the cabin. Right?"

"Right!" we cheered.

I could see what Andie was getting at. No makeup, who cared? If we acted like it didn't matter—which it didn't—we were actually defeating the guys' attempt to aggravate us. Perfect!

"Hey, you know something?" Amy-Liz said. "We don't have to mess with primping. And it's not because our makeup's gone."

I knew what she was getting at. "Because we don't wanna attract guys anyway, right?"

"Bingo," Andie said.

I couldn't help thinking that Jared, Billy, and Stan had more smarts than to risk being sent home for ripping off our sports bags. But then again, they were behaving like males, so maybe their smarts had gone ker-plooey!

Kayla still looked frantic. "We can't wait too long to locate our things," she said. "I simply must have my makeup by supper."

"You'll be fine without it," I reassured her. "Just look at the rest of us."

Paula wasn't taking this business of zero makeup nearly as hard as Kayla. Not long ago, though, she would've been freaking out right along with her twin. Thanks to an afternoon at my house, Paula had seen the light. She had abandoned her mascara-laden eyelashes. The heavy rouge, too.

When it came right down to it, Paula's natural look enhanced her true beauty. It did something else, too. Her fresh, clean look set her apart from Kayla. It gave her a new identity—her very own. Except now, the two of them looked exactly alike.

"Couldn't I at least borrow from another girl somewhere?" Kayla asked sheepishly. This was a major concession from a girl who wore only designer clothes and used the most expensive makeup on the market.

"Listen, if it comes down to the wire, Kayla, you're welcome to beg makeup from the girls in Cabin A," Andie offered. "But"—and here she let her mischievous side surface—"if you do, you're out of the S.O.S."

Kayla's face drooped.

"Andie's kidding," I said, grinning. "But really, if

none of us wears makeup, no one will stick out." I was hoping to soften the blow for Kayla.

"Besides, you don't wanna attract guys this week anyway, remember?" Andie teased.

Paula patted her twin's shoulder. "If you did, you'd just have to turn around and ignore them."

We laughed at that, heading to our cabin wrapped in beach towels—feeling smug about not letting the loss of some petty things like makeup and a change of clothes spoil our afternoon.

S.O.S. rules!

It did seem kind of weird not putting on even a touch of makeup after showering, though. Mom would never believe I went to supper bare-faced! I remembered a zillion times when I'd fought to wear it. But here at camp with the pact, things were much different.

That evening we had a cookout featuring barbecued chicken, corn on the cob, baked beans, and watermelon for dessert.

In line, Jared took one look at us and burst out laughing. "What's this . . . the natural look?"

"Right," Stan said. "So natural, you don't wanna look!"

The guys howled with laughter. Except Todd. He sat there in the middle of it all, surrounded by a pack of ignorant Dressel Hills males, behaving like a perfectly wonderful gentleman. Man, what our guys could learn from a Buena Vista cowboy!

None of us were moved by the ridicule. We were as cool as cucumbers.

After supper, all the campers hiked the half-mile

into Ouray. The whole time, we ignored the boys, but they kept bugging us anyway. Stan untied Andie's shoelaces while she read a brochure, but she kept her nose up and completely ignored him. Jared bumped into Shauna "accidentally" when we stopped for ice cream, knocking the ice cream out of her cone. She simply picked it up, tossed it in the trash can, and went inside to order another one. By the time we headed down the street to the San Juan Jeep Company, the guys were totally mystified.

Mr. Boyce and the counselors collected some brochures. And after they conferred together, Rhonna told us we were scheduled to go on the wildest jeep trip of all—the Black Bear—next Wednesday, the last full day of camp!

Before heading back, we were allowed to split up for one hour. Several groups of guys headed for the Buckskin Trading Co., a store specializing in history books and mining. Danny and several other studious types made a beeline for a bookstore called Food For Thought. Jared and Stan followed us girls around, taunting us about being in public without our "faces" on. After a full thirty minutes of no response, they got bored and left. At last!

We wandered from one specialty shop to another. Then I saw it. Dozens of brightly colored shirts filled the window, and wild, neon lights spelled out: *The You-Name-It T-Shirt Shop*.

"Come on, girls!" I called, gesturing toward the store.

"What's up?" Shauna asked.

"I don't wear T-shirts," Kayla sniffed.

But I dragged them over to the shop anyway. I had a brainstorm.

"Here's my idea," I said, once all the sisters were gathered around me. "How about if we get matching pink T-shirts with the letters S.O.S. on the front!"

"And let's put a picture of a guy on the back, X'd out," Andie joked.

We all laughed. But—"Too obvious," I said. "This way, with only the letters on the front, the guys'll never know about our secret society. Besides, it will drive them crazy trying to figure it out!"

"As if they weren't going crazy already," Shauna observed.

We laughed, rejoicing over our successful strategy.

"What shade of pink?" Kayla asked. "Fuchsia goes best with my skin tone." Surprisingly, she seemed excited about the idea—even though the shirts weren't super expensive.

"How about this one?" Shauna pulled a pink shirt from the stacks on the shelf and held it up.

"Nice," Paula approved.

Then I noticed Amy-Liz hanging back from the rest of us. She caught my eye, then said bravely, "Sorry, girls, you go ahead, but I can't get a shirt."

"Why not?" Andie said without thinking. Then she remembered and blushed. We all looked at each other, embarrassed.

"I have some extra cash," Paula volunteered, opening her tiny shoulder purse.

Amy-Liz freaked out. "If I can't afford it, that's my problem."

"But you're in the society," Shauna argued. "You *have* to have a matching shirt."

"It's okay, really," Amy-Liz insisted. But it wasn't okay, and I could see this whole thing escalating. Whew, it was a good thing she didn't know how the church had gotten the money for her camp scholarship!

"We'll just forget the whole idea," I said.

"Look," Amy-Liz said, sitting down. "I'm not going to spoil everyone's fun. Go ahead, get the shirts. I insist!"

Kayla's eyes sparkled. "Listen, Amy," she began. "What if I loan the money to you?"

Amy-Liz stared at the floor.

I held my breath.

"You can pay me back later," Kayla said. Wisely, she waited before digging into her wallet.

It was fabulous—Amy-Liz agreed!

Chattering excitedly, we headed to the counter to place our order. Fuchsia pink shirts with white letters. S.O.S.!

"Hey, let's change into them now!" Amy-Liz suggested. So we took turns using the tiny dressing room to change into our shirts, stuffing our old shirts into the plastic bags they'd given us.

The hike back to camp was a blast. Everyone, even the other girls from our church, asked us what S.O.S. meant. But it was the guys who bugged us the most. When we didn't give them answers, Jared came up with his own solution. "S.O.S. Yeah, these girls need help, all right," he said loud enough for everyone to hear.

My sisters and I laughed right along with those foolish boys. If only they knew!

SEVENTEEN

Back at camp, we undressed for bed, recounting the T-shirt episode, careful not to divulge anything to Rhonna, who was definitely listening. I could tell she knew that something was up, but she was being awful cool about not prying.

Shauna volunteered to sleep on the floor. "If it's okay with you," she said, "I'll trade permanently."

I was surprised. "How come?"

She looked sheepish. "Well, if you wanna know the truth, I'm not comfortable up there." She pointed to the bunk above Joy's bed. "I'm afraid I'll fall off the bunk and hit my head—get a concussion or something."

No one laughed. We could see she wasn't kidding.

"Sure, I'll trade," I said. "But what about Joy? You two are best friends." I glanced at Andie, who was already snuggling down for the night. "Maybe Andie and Joy could trade, too," I suggested—which they did after a quick change of sheets and blankets.

So . . . Joy slept in the lower bunk beside Shauna, who crawled into the sleeping bag on the floor, and that was settled. Well, almost. None of us really settled down until Rhonna started devotions.

She began by reading the Golden Rule. "'In everything,'"—she emphasized *everything*—"'do to others what you would have them do to you, for this sums up the Law and the Prophets.'"

I felt strange. Guilty, I guess. We sure weren't treating the guys the way Jesus had commanded us to. But they'd treated us pretty lousy in the first place, I thought, justifying our actions in my mind.

Rhonna continued. "All of us are unique in God's eyes. We're made in his image. Just because certain people are different doesn't mean we should decide they're inferior."

I wondered how much Rhonna had been listening to our conversations.

Andie blurted, "But what do you do when guys act like . . ." She stopped, looking at me. I could tell she was struggling with how much to share.

Rhonna finished Andie's sentence. "When *certain* guys act like jerks?" She smiled knowingly. "*All* guys aren't jerks, Andie, if that's what you mean."

It was exactly what Andie meant.

"Certain guys is right." Andie groaned.

Rhonna grinned. "Let me tell you a story—a true story—about when I was your age."

You could almost hear a collective sigh. An interested sigh, that is. We leaned back on our pillows, our hands supporting our heads as we listened to Rhonna tell about her past.

"There was a boy," she began. "A *very* fine boy."

We giggled. Rhonna was so cool.

"His name was Mel, and he was the heartthrob of the youth group." She stopped, like she was thinking ahead to the good part. "Only thing, Mel was prejudiced. Prejudiced against slanted-eyed girls like me. He even had a nickname for me. Honestly, I've forgotten it now. Maybe I blocked it out of my memory because it was so painful."

I was beginning to feel sorry for Rhonna.

She continued, "One night after church, I tried to introduce myself, to let him know I actually had a name. He turned away from me and started talking to some other girl . . . like I barely existed. Well, later my older sister found out through the grapevine that he refused to have anything to do with Orientals."

"Why?" Amy-Liz asked, wide-eyed.

Rhonna shrugged. "Some people can't accept others who look different from them. It's sad, but true. But just because Mel was a jerk didn't mean that *all* the guys in my youth group were in the same category."

Andie smiled. "So you're saying that just because certain guys bug us doesn't mean we should shut 'em all out?"

Yeah, Andie, I thought. My mind was on Todd. Again.

Rhonna nodded. "Some boys take a longer time to grow up, I guess you could say. But by ignoring the obnoxious ones—which you all did very well"—she grinned knowingly—"you are showing them you can't be hurt by their antics."

131

"So," I piped up, "you think we did the right thing by ignoring them?"

There was a mischievous sparkle in her eyes. "Just don't turn it into some organized society or something. In other words, don't carry things too far."

I gasped. It sounded like she knew about S.O.S.!

I glanced around at my sisters. For once, we were really earning our name. The sisters were solemn—and silent.

❤   ❤   ❤

The next morning at breakfast, I noticed several Buena Vista girls casting snooty glances from the next table. A short redhead was one of them.

I decided to ignore them—something I was getting better and better at all the time.

Most the guys had cleared out when Miss Carrot Tops strutted up to our table. It seemed she had planned her strategy well, since she waited for Rhonna to excuse herself before showing up.

"You don't know me." She smiled a mixture of braces and lip gloss. "I'm Laina Springer, Cabin E."

I forced a smile, trying to be cordial.

Laina leaned down, whispering. "The guys from your church are scheming something low-down dirty."

"Like what kind of low-down dirty?" I asked.

"I . . . uh, we heard it was something about getting someone's attention." Springer's braces twinkled momentarily.

"Who said?" I asked.

She fidgeted, looking around at her friends still sitting at the table behind ours. "Well, according to Billy Hill,"—and with the mention of his name her face burst into a wide grin—"your church guys are ticked off. So they've got some big surprise planned."

Andie shot up out of her seat. "What sorta surprise?"

"Beats me," Laina said, turning to leave. "Just thought you'd wanna know."

Yeah, right! I wasn't going to let *her* scare me.

"Listen, Laina." I reached out to touch her arm. "We really appreciate the tip. Thanks a lot." I forced the biggest, most sincere smile I could conjure up. "Oh, and if you happen to hear anything else, could you let us know?"

Her shiny lips twisted over her braces into a weird little pained expression. "Sure," she peeped out and returned to her table.

What was the guys' motive in giving us this advanced warning? Maybe they planned to get us all freaked out, on the edge of our seats anticipating something drastic. And then, absolutely nothing would happen.

I pondered these thoughts for a moment. Then quickly, before Rhonna returned, I shared my theory with the rest of the S.O.S.

Andie frowned. "Surely the guys aren't *that* stupid. I mean, just look at the trouble they could get into just from taking our makeup and stuff."

Paula eyeballed Laina Springer and the girls at the other table. "I can't believe Billy would tell her."

"Well, *I* can," Amy-Liz interrupted.

And so could I.

Kayla looked a little foggy, like she wasn't so sure about all this.

Amy-Liz set down her lemonade glass. "You know, Holly might be onto something. Maybe we oughta keep watch."

"I'm still trying to figure what makes guys tick," Andie said.

Paula fluffed her bangs. "If Holly's right, this would be one way for the guys to ruin our week without doing a single thing."

Kayla nodded, like the light had finally dawned. "Sounds feasible."

I grinned. "It's the coward's way to get us guarding our cabin door."

Shauna sat up. "If you wanna know the truth, I think Jared's still mad because Holly broke up with him."

"Well, we mustn't let it spoil our camp experience," Kayla commented.

"Kayla's right," I said, grateful to see Laina and friends get up and carry their trays off to the kitchen. Followed by her string of straight-faced girlfriends, the spunky redhead looked like a contemporary pied piper. I couldn't imagine Billy linking up with the likes of her. But Billy Hill, just like his cohorts, was the epitome of an unpredictable male.

Another busy day sped by.

Swimming, craft classes, a noon-time picnic, horse-back riding, and finally the twilight hike. Not once did any of the make-up-less S.O.S. speak to a guy. Not a single time!

After supper, we headed off on our hike with Rhonna.

Several other girls and their counselors joined us, but fortunately, not Cabin E.

I was looking forward to this hike. I figured since I had given up guys, the least I could do was enjoy the rest of God's creation. Sunsets included.

Rhonna insisted that each of us carry a water bottle in our backpacks, as well as granola bars and flashlights, even though we were only going for a moderate hike. She was like that. "Be prepared for anything," she said.

Steadily, we worked our way up a gradual incline, stopping occasionally to catch our breath and view the sights, hearts pounding from exertion. Andie and I linked up as hiking partners, and even though lately Paula wasn't too eager to hang out with her twin, she teamed up with Kayla automatically.

Rhonna and Joy led the way, with Shauna and Amy-Liz close behind. The trail was wide enough for two to walk side-by-side.

"This trail will adjust us gradually to the altitude," Rhonna said when we paused for one of our huff-and-puff stops.

"How high up are we, anyway?" Joy asked.

"Almost eight thousand feet," Rhonna said.

"Whew!" Andie whistled.

I sat down on a log to tie my tennies and catch my breath. Suddenly, out of the stillness came a high-pitched whistle. I leaped off the log. "What's that?"

Rhonna chuckled. "Sounds like a marmot just saying hello."

Andie searched everywhere for the furry little guy, but the rodent must have scurried off to his burrow for the night.

I squinted as the Saturday sun sank behind the mountains beyond us to the west. "Look, Andie, it's almost sunset," I said, enjoying the peaceful moments of early evening. What a fabulous contrast to the conflict of the first three days at camp.

We hiked farther before stopping midway up one of the highest mountains overlooking Ouray. Andie and I found a place to sit on a massive rock at the edge of the trail. There, I stared in awe at the sunset. Reds and golds streaked the western sky, and the sweet smell of pine filled the air. In the hushed stillness of twilight, the S.O.S., the pact, and the hassles with boys disappeared.

After a long silence, Rhonna whispered, "Girls, look!"

Far below in an open meadow, a deer meandered from the protection of the pine forest, searching for cool mountain waters. I held my breath as she located the stream and drank.

Rhonna said softly, "'As the deer pants for streams of water, so my soul pants for you, O God.'"

I recognized the psalm she quoted. It was one of Mom's favorites. For a split second, I wished Jared and Billy, and the other guys—Danny too—could have been here to witness the inspiring scene. Ripping off makeup and making "low-down dirty" threats might seem insignificant at a time like this.

After the hike, we headed back to our cabins, ready for a full night's sleep. I wondered if the guys had pulled a fast one while we were gone—that deed our weaselly informant had warned us about at supper. But as we crossed the log bridge leading to Cabin B, things appeared to be perfectly normal.

"Nothin' happened," Andie whispered as we rummaged around for our toothbrushes and towels.

"Let's hope it stays that way," I replied.

Andie and I were the first to make the nightly trek to the bathroom. "Here, we'll need this," she said, pulling a flashlight out of her backpack.

When we arrived, Andie pointed her flashlight into the darkened log structure. "Anyone home?" she called out. I giggled as she groped for a light switch.

Nothing.

Again she tried the lights.

"Something's wrong," she said. "The electricity must be off."

A quick glance toward the dining hall/chapel building told us differently. "That's weird, lights are on everywhere but up here," I said.

"Well, whatever's wrong, I can't wait forever," she stated. "You guard the door, and I'll take the flashlight with me." Andie hummed a song of courage as she disappeared into the darkness.

Outhouses and outdoor rest rooms had never been favorite places for me. Maybe one reason was because I had gotten locked inside a nasty-smelling outhouse on the top of Copper Mountain last summer.

Andie's humming stopped. The night was too still.

I inched forward. "Andie?"

"I can't believe this," she wailed. "There's no toilet paper!"

"I'll go find some," I said, bravely entering the darkness to aid my friend. When I made the turn into the stall area, my eyes became better adjusted thanks to Andie's flashlight. I opened the door to the stall beside hers.

No paper.

I went to the next one, and the next. "How bizarre. Do you think the camp maintenance people forgot to restock?"

"Oh, this is great," Andie said with a sigh. "Remember what that Laina Springer said about the guys?"

I gasped. "It *is* them. This is despicable!"

"So, what am I gonna do?"

"Wait here," I said. "I'll get some tissues."

On my way back to the cabin, I met up with the other girls. Quickly, I filled them in on the situation. Hearing the news, the Sisters grew more determined than ever to ignore the boys.

Amy-Liz summed it up for all of us. "One thing's for sure," she said, "if this is how the guys think they're gonna get our attention, they're still *absolutely* wrong!"

❤   ❤   ❤

Later, while lying in bed, I thought of the events of the day. If taking light bulbs and toilet paper was the low-down dirty deed Laina had mentioned, then the rest of camp week was going to be a cinch.

Still, I wondered how the guys would respond to

zero reaction from us girls. Would they become even more determined to get our attention?

Joy and Shauna were still whispering as I gave in to the scratchy feeling behind my eyes. I dreamed a marmot was chasing me, but when I woke up, I realized the sound of the marmot's whistle was coming from Andie's stuffy nose.

Sometime later, in the misty, wee hours, I was sure I heard people tiptoeing around in the cabin. Cracking open my eyes, I saw someone's braces gleam in the moonlight. But when I tried to sit up, my body went stiff as a board. Absolutely numb. The sleep stupor overtook me, and I sank into it.

Rhonna's alarm rang too early the next morning. I fell back to sleep. Much later, I woke up to the sound of Paula and Kayla whispering. I opened one eye and saw them gather up their towels and clean clothes for the day. Without makeup, they looked identical. The twins headed out the front door.

I squinted my other eye open, yawning. Looking around, I saw that Andie and I were the only ones left in the cabin. Joy, Amy-Liz, and Shauna must have wanted to be the first to hit the showers.

I peeled dead skin off my arm while relaxing on my upper bunk. Wide awake now, I leaned over the side, peeking down at Andie. She looked so little all curled up in a ball beneath me. I was proud of her stand against my brousin, even though I knew it was painful. After all, Stan had been the longest-running boyfriend Andie ever had.

I stretched in my bunk, eager for another busy day at camp.

The twins hadn't been gone more than five minutes when I heard Kayla yelling. "Those horrible boys!"

"Holly! Andie!" Paula called as she came back into the cabin.

I tossed off the covers. "Wha-at?"

"Come look," Kayla said, peeking her head into the cabin. "You'll never believe this!"

Andie appeared unconcerned. She rolled over, pulled the blankets over her head, and snoozed on.

I swung down off the top bunk, then grabbed my bathrobe and pulled it on as fast as I could. In my bare feet, I ran out the door and down the path behind Paula and Kayla.

When we came to the clearing at the bottom of the slope, I stopped cold in my tracks. Directly in front of the chapel stood three stately pine trees, uniquely decorated. Their branches displayed underwear—pink, blue, and white bras, matching panties, and two pairs of baby-doll pajamas.

An underwear raid!

And not just *any* underwear raid. I could see Andie's iron-on name tags adorning numerous items. Paula and Kayla's bras were obvious by their size. My own lingerie was recognizable, of course. At least, by me.

"Low-down dirty, all right," I said, completely stunned. "How embarrassing."

Kayla and Paula stared in silence.

"We've got to get this stuff down before breakfast," I said. "Mr. Boyce will have a cow!"

"Shouldn't the guys be worried about that?" Paula asked.

"You'd think so, but once again, we're not dealing with intelligence here," I reminded them.

We hurried back to the cabin. Thank goodness we'd discovered this bright and early!

"Andie!" I hollered, out of breath. "Get up!"

She moaned pitifully from her mound of covers. I pounced on her bed. "C'mon, Andie. This is war!"

"What's war?" she muttered in a sleepy, throaty voice.

Such a way to begin the Lord's day.

EIGHTEEN

Andie got up immediately when I announced that her baby doll pajamas were waving in the breeze in front of the chapel.

Just then Shauna, Joy, and Amy-Liz arrived back from the showers, their hair still damp. "What's going on?" Joy said when she saw our faces.

Paula explained the situation, and panic ensued.

"Not my expensive bras!" Kayla moaned.

"You think you have it bad. My underwear is *labeled*!" Andie complained.

"The guys are begging for war," I said.

In nothing flat, all of us were standing in front of those three pine trees. Paula reached up, trying to retrieve her dangling blue bra.

"Our guys, all right. Had to be," Andie fumed. "But let's deal with who did it later. We need some long-handled brooms . . . or something."

Amy-Liz found a rake around the side of the girls'

rest room and shower area. "Too convenient, don'tcha think?"

I wondered about that, too. Had the guys actually come into our cabin and used this rake to do their wretched deed?

"Wish we could dust for fingerprints," Andie said, eyeing the rake handle.

"No kidding." I watched as the Miller twins carefully located their personal items, getting them down with the long rake handle.

One after another, we stretched and strained, poking at pine branches with the rake, bobbing for underwear. Andie was last. She was too short to reach her baby doll pajamas and panties and things. I volunteered to help while the rest of the girls headed off to the cabin.

"We can't let the guys get away with this," she hissed.

I agreed, shoving the Golden Rule out of my mind. "I have a plan."

"Good, because if you don't, I do!"

It turned out that the entire S.O.S.—once we were gathered in the cabin—was in agreement with my plan. We would deliver a declaration of war describing why we were retaliating and what we wanted. It all boiled down to this: the guys wanted our attention. Well, they would get it. I scribbled furiously.

> *This is a declaration of war!*
> *We, the girls in Cabin B, do declare war on the boys at Camp Ouray. You have taken our personal items and displayed them disrespectfully for the world to see. You have stolen our makeup and*

clothing. You have hurt our feelings and tampered
with our self-esteem.

   Therefore, we declare all-out war. Starting from
the second this envelope is opened. In return, we
want respect. From all of you!

> *Signed,*
> *Holly, Shauna, Andie, Joy,*
> *Amy-Liz, Paula, Kayla*

Andie was chomping at the bit as she signed—no, scribbled—her name. Kayla could hardly write her name, she was so angry.

When all of us had signed the document, I added a P.S. at the bottom: *The Bible says, "There is a time for everything. A time for war and a time for peace." Well, guess what time it is!*

I folded the paper and put it into one of my stationery envelopes. "I'll deliver this," I said grimly, waving it in the air.

On my way to the camp post office, I ran into Todd.

"Holly!" he called to me.

"Oh, hi," I said. *Perfect timing!* "Could you give something to someone for me?" I said sweetly, then realized how perfectly insensible that sounded.

"Sure," he said, glancing at the envelope in my hand. "Like who?"

"Uh, you know Jared Wilkins, right?"

He nodded.

I handed Todd the war letter. "Thanks a lot," I said, dying for Jared to read it and spread the word.

He frowned. "What's this about? You two are really fighting, aren't you?"

"Uh, not just him and me," I explained. "The girls

in Cabin B have had it with the entire male camp population."

He looked stunned. "Why? What happened?"

I turned to go. "It's a *long* story."

"Wait, Holly, about the Talent Night...." He looked serious. "Have you decided on anything yet?"

No way was he going to fit into the scheme of things. Not *this* summer.

"Maybe you should ask someone else," I said. "Sorry, but thanks for delivering the letter. See ya." I waved and was off before he could pursue the matter. I wasn't too thrilled about conversing with the enemy, polite—and cute—or not! As far as my sisters and I were concerned, there was no neutral ground with our war strategy.

It was all-out war, beginning with water balloons to be administered during Quiet Time, right after the noon meal. Over lunch, we drew up our battle plans.

Andie wanted to blow a trumpet or something and march around the boys' cabin.

"You've gotta be out of your mind," I said.

"Yeah," Amy-Liz agreed, pushing down her bright orange socks. "We'll attract too much attention."

"Okay, then what?" Andie asked, looking too eager to embark on the first attack.

I made a quick sketch of the boys' cabin area, showing the route we could take—down the steep slope, through the pine forest, around the amphitheater, and up the hill.

"Masterful," Kayla said, tracing the imaginary path with her well-manicured finger.

Instead of Joshua's army, we were the S.O.S. battalion.

❤   ❤   ❤

Our initial attack was so fabulous! We never even looked where we were throwing. Just opened the guys' cabin door and pelted those boys but good!

At first, they yelled. Then their shouts turned to enthusiastic hooting as some of the balloons came flying back in our direction.

Shaving cream, too.

The cabin was filled with white foam, spilling out through the doorway, hissing through the screened windows. What an unexpected counter attack!

Kayla screamed. Some of the shaving cream caught her in the eye, and Paula guided her away from the chaos, towards the girls' rest room.

"Retreat!" Andie shouted, and all of us followed.

Our Quiet Time officially ended with us explaining a few things to Rhonna before devotions. Of course, we left out the part about a zillion water balloons and where we'd been. Fortunately, we'd rinsed off the shaving cream before returning.

Paying attention to Rhonna's devotional and her prayer wasn't easy with my mind on our next strategy conference. Even so, I heard snatches of words like: overlooking wrong deeds, forgiveness, getting along, etcetera.

Later, Andie got the bright idea to ask permission for us to take a short hike. Without Rhonna. It was free time, anyway.

Rhonna agreed. She looked worn out; probably

from all those early jogging sessions. Surely it had nothing to do with keeping track of seven conniving females.

When we were far enough away from the cabin, our meeting began under the covering of the pine forest.

"What happened back there?" Kayla asked, referring to the guys' ammunition.

"Yeah, where'd the shaving cream come from?" Shauna complained.

I shrugged. "They must've planned to launch an attack of their own."

"Well, we beat 'em to it!" Andie cheered.

Paula touched her damp bangs. "What's next?"

"Tomorrow morning—early—we get 'em good," I said.

Andie grinned. "Yes!"

"We'll get up really early. When the guys take their showers, we'll be hiding outside, around the back, waiting to turn off the hot water."

Joy looked uneasy. "Do all of us have to?"

"We're in this together, right?" I said.

"S.O.S.," said Andie, "S.O.S."

Eagerly, we picked up the chant, heading to inspect the pipe system outside the girls' rest room. Afterwards, I sneaked through the trees behind the guys' rest room and studied the pipe system there.

Perfect! They were identical.

❤   ❤   ❤

None of us thought we'd sleep that night, but we were wrong. Not only do camp schedules wear you out, kids sleep better after inhaling clean mountain air all day. That's what Rhonna said, anyway.

I had set my watch alarm for six-thirty.

Please, Lord, let Rhonna jog tomorrow, I prayed silently as I fell into bed.

God must've answered my prayer.

Monday morning, Rhonna was long gone when my watch began to play its wake-up tune. Ten minutes later, Andie and Paula were on either side of me, aiming their flashlights into a network of pipes and spigots outside the boys' shower area.

"That's not it," I whispered, searching for the hot water pipe.

"Where *is* it?" Andie hissed. "Remember where we found it behind our rest room? Think!"

I envisioned the identical setup behind our rest rooms.

"We've gotta find it!" Paula said, glancing at Kayla.

"Hold the flashlight still!" I ordered my assistants. "There"—my eyes scanned the pipes once again—"I think that's it."

"We'll know soon enough," Amy-Liz said, crouching down.

"Who's going to stand post?" I asked.

Shauna volunteered. Silently, she headed to a clump of aspen trees around the side of the log cabin structure. It was the perfect hiding place, especially in the pre-dawn light.

The early risers, Jared and Danny, headed inside the small building first, followed soon by Billy and Stan. We'd assigned numbers to the boys so that whoever stood post could flash the appropriate fingers to the rest of us behind the building. Jared was number one, Stan number two, and so on.

The gentle rumble of pressure pushing through the outside pipes told us the water was on. We could hear the guys' talking their easy-going, early-morning, boring nonsense. Probably soaping up . . .

We waited a few more seconds.

"Ready . . . set . . . now!" Andie said.

I turned the hot-water spigot all the way. Hard.

Off!

Howling followed. Loud, freaking howls.

"Let's go!" I whispered.

Shauna dashed over to catch up with us.

"Outta here!" Andie said as we flew up the dirt path, across the log bridge, and into the safety of our cabin.

"Listen!" Amy-Liz said, standing in the doorway.

"Can you hear them?" I strained, listening.

"It's most likely your imagination," Paula said.

We stood by the window grinning.

"What a horrible thing to do," Joy said.

Yet we grinned long after the deed was done.

NINETEEN

The guys sent a delegation—Jared and Stan—to talk to Andie and me during lunch. The four of us moved to a vacant table with our trays. It seemed strange having an extended conversation with guys like this.

Jared got things started. "If it's respect you want, let's talk."

"So talk." Andie wasn't making it easy for the guys' first attempt at a peace conference.

"Okay," Jared said, winking at me. "How about getting back together?"

"That's not what this is about!" Andie piped up. "Don't you guys pay attention at all?"

Stan looked puzzled. "We're here to talk peace," he reprimanded Jared. "The thing about going out can wait till later."

"Just a minute!" I said. "Are you saying this peace thing hinges on people getting back together?"

Jared ran his fingers through his dark waves. "You could say that."

Andie stood up. "Then forget it!" She motioned to me, and we picked up our trays.

"Hey, girl, you want your makeup or not?" Stan taunted.

"Keep it!" Andie called over her shoulder.

But Jared and Stan didn't return to their table. They followed us to our table, focusing on Amy-Liz.

"I need to talk to you, Amy," Jared said, shooting a sly glance at me.

Amy-Liz turned to look at me. "What's this about?"

"Why don't you just go away, Jared," Andie said. She was as nervous as I was.

Jared stood his ground. "We *have* to talk, Amy-Liz."

"Leave me alone," she said, turning her shoulder to him.

Jared's eyes danced. Sneery like. "It's about your camp scholarship."

No, not that!

The S.O.S. gasped in unison.

Amy-Liz frowned. "What about it?"

Jared leaned closer to her. "Let me be the first to tell you where the money really came from!"

All seven of us squirmed while Jared enjoyed himself to the hilt. Amy's face got white. She looked first at Jared, then at Andie and me. "What's he talking about?"

Before I could respond, Jared took her by the arm. "I think you'd better come with me," he said.

Horrified, we watched as Amy-Liz left us to go sit with the archenemy at a table near the dessert window. "The war rages on," I said, worried about the consequences of Jared's deed. This would surely be the demise of the Sisters of Silence. And Jared knew it.

"We might as well kiss Amy-Liz good-bye," Andie said mournfully.

"You can say that again," Paula said. "Remember how she freaked when we tried to give her money for our S.O.S. T-shirts?"

Kayla sighed. "Not only that, but she'll get her makeup back, you watch!" No one laughed even though Kayla's remark was funny in a sad sort of way.

"Do you think she'll leave camp?" Shauna asked.

Joy looked wistful. "I hope she doesn't."

I shook my head. "Amy's probably so upset right this minute, who knows what she's thinking or saying?" And I had no doubt Jared would worm the secret society information right out of her.

"Hey, wait a minute," Andie said, gawking at them. "Check it out."

I couldn't believe my eyes. Amy-Liz was marching back to our table, her face shining! Jared, on the other hand, sat alone with a dejected look on his usually cheerful face.

"Interesting," I said. "Now let's see what she says."

Amy-Liz started hugging Andie and me. "You did that . . . you baked all those cookies so I could come?"

She was blubbering all over us about what we had done. Whew, what a relief!

Once again, the guys' attempt to destroy our unity had failed. We were stronger than ever!

❤   ❤   ❤

Hours after Lights Out, the S.O.S. found some bowls in the camp kitchen. After filling them with warm water, we tiptoed to the boys' cabin area.

Since Jared was my target, and Stan, Andie's, the two of us crept inside first. If all went well, Paula would dish out the hand-in-warm-water trick to Billy, Kayla's target was Danny, and the rest of the girls would stand guard outside.

We were so good, we never even made a sound. We were Silent Sisters, all right!

Jared's right hand went willingly into the bowl. Quickly, I left the cabin and hid behind a tree with Paula, waiting for Andie.

Soon, she emerged. Victory!

One by one, the girls administered the prank. Miraculously, we pulled it off.

The next morning I wrote in my journal. *Tuesday, June 28th: We did it! We pulled off a major, I mean MAJOR, attack last night. I still can't believe we didn't get caught!*

Tomorrow morning's the jeep trip. We're going to experience hairpin turns and switch-backs. I can't wait! After that, we'll come back to camp for a wiener roast, and then . . . Talent Night!

I still don't know what I'm doing for my talent. Todd

Stillson wants me to sing a duet with him, but that's impossible. Too bad things turned out this way.

How I wish I could've been a little mouse hiding somewhere in Jared's cabin this morning. Man, I'll bet those boys were ticked! When they see the bowls of water, they'll know the truth. The S.O.S. doesn't mess around!

More later.

Bed sheets were hanging out of every single one of Jared's cabin windows! We honestly tried not to giggle about it on our way to breakfast. It was mean, what we had done, but a powerful message had been sent. Maybe as strong a message as we girls had ever sent!

After lunch we swam in the pool, just us girls. The guys had gone into Ouray to the hot springs pool.

So ... it was a complete mystery when a white Flag of Truce found its way into the ground beside my beach towel.

"Hey, look at this," I said to my dripping, shivering sisters. Reaching down, I read the note pinned to the makeshift flag.

Andie peered at the note as I read it. "Looks like they bit the dust," she cackled. "They want to end the war!"

"And check this out," I said, laughing. "They're calling for 'a time of peace'! They actually want to meet and have a talk."

"Oh wow, a pow-wow," Amy-Liz said, and we cracked up.

"So, when do we talk?" Joy asked.

"The note suggests we meet the guys after the

campfire, in front of the three pine trees," I said. "Everyone agree?"

"Sounds fine to me," Shauna said.

"Let's wait for the guys to do the talking," I suggested. "We'll see how sorry they really are."

We hurried off to the showers, wondering what would happen after the campfire.

After supper was a volleyball tournament—boys against the girls. We played Cabin D the first game. And then—we had to play Jared's cabin.

Groan.

"C'mon, girls, let's show 'em," Andie said.

The game turned out great. Strong competition . . . the works. Almost like a real war!

Except for one thing: the opponents, especially— Jared, Stan, and Billy—were being super nice. Giving us the benefit of the doubt during the game. Concerned when one of us tripped and fell. Stuff like that. They weren't letting us win, though. I wondered why.

In the end, we got creamed—21 to 4. Jared and Billy came up afterwards and shook hands just like in professional sports. Stan hung around Andie and me, behaving like a cool stepbrother . . . and friend. It didn't even bug me when he turned on the John Wayne charm!

When it got dark, we built a campfire and sat around singing. Rhonna passed out marshmallows, and our guys offered sticks to roast them. I accepted the offer from Jared and watched as he used his pocket knife to sharpen the end. I marveled at his change of spirit. He even *looked* repentant.

During devotions, Pastor Rob talked to us about unity within the family of God. I wondered, had someone spilled the beans? Did he know about the war?

"What kind of important info can we learn from Romans 12:16 today?" Pastor Rob asked.

Danny raised his hand. "That we should 'live in harmony with one another.'"

Pastor Rob slowly made eye contact with each of us around the campfire. "What does that mean for you and me?"

Laina Springer raised her hand. "I guess we're supposed to try and get along." She glanced sheepishly at me.

Pastor Rob nodded. "That's right. Now jumping down to verses eighteen and nineteen"—he shone a flashlight on his New Testament—"'If it is possible, as far as it depends on you, live at peace with everyone. Do not take revenge, my friends, but leave room for God's wrath, for it is written: It is mine to avenge; I will repay, says the Lord.'"

I could hardly swallow as I listened to Pastor Rob. What he was saying hit home. Hard. We had treated the guys—our own brothers in Christ—like enemies! The pact, and the war, too, were wrong. The boys had treated us poorly, true, but we'd carried things too far.

Long before the coals died out in the campfire, I was ready to talk peace. And talk we did. We met the guys at the pre-appointed spot. Silently, they piled the sports bags in front of us.

How desperately I wanted to erase the memory of

my underwear rippling in the breeze. Could I forgive the boys for that embarrassment?

"Okay, who wants to start?" Danny asked, looking around.

I took a deep breath, ready to speak, but Joy beat me to it. "I'm sorry for ignoring you guys all week." She coughed nervously. "It was wrong."

"I'm sorry, too," Billy confessed, "about setting up Laina and her friends to raid your cabin."

"Laina did your dirty work?" I said, a little confused. Then I remembered. I *had* seen her braces in the moonlight!

Paula stepped forward, looking at Danny. "I'm really sorry about making you wet your bed." She was sincere, but we girls burst out giggling.

Danny turned beet red. I could see it even in the fading light of dusk. "Don't ever do that again," he said softly.

"You're supposed to forgive her, Danny," I teased. "Practice what you preach."

Jared turned to me and apologized for taking my hair band. "And I didn't mean it about your hair," he said, moving closer. "I love your hair, Holly-Heart. Honest."

"Uh, oh," Andie muttered while the rest of my sisters groaned audibly.

Jared gave me a quick hug. It was sweet, and reminded me of Andie's twin brothers when they'd hugged and made up after their sand fight.

I couldn't contain myself. "The S.O.S. was my idea," I confessed. "So was the pact. I guess we got a little carried away."

Jared looked puzzled. "What was S.O.S. supposed to mean, anyway?" he asked.

"Sisters of Silence," I said.

"Oh . . . yeah," he said, thinking it through. "You were silent, all right."

"Maybe talking things out would've been better," Andie said.

"No kidding," Stan admitted.

Danny fidgeted.

"Well, what's it gonna be?" Andie asked. "Forgiven or not?"

The guys looked at each other. Jared shrugged. "Okay."

Stan said, "Forgiven."

Billy agreed, "Wiped out of my mind."

Danny piped up: "Hey, there's a really cool verse about forgiveness I memorized just today."

"Whoa, Danny, you're avoiding the subject," Jared said. He shot a look at Stan and Billy. And—as if they'd planned it hours earlier—they promptly picked up "Preacher Danny" and hauled him down the slope to the cold mountain stream.

I could still hear Danny yelling for mercy as we picked up our sports bags and made our way back to good ol' Cabin B.

But it didn't take me long to forget about our church boys. Because I was already plotting what I would say the next time I saw Todd Stillson.

TWENTY

"I feel like a new person," I told Andie later that night. She was at the sink next to me applying makeup like crazy. "And it has nothing to do with this." I studied my mascara brush.

Andie glanced at me in the mirror. "You're right." She sighed. "Just think, we almost messed up our entire week with that stupid war."

I curled my eyelashes and applied a light layer of dark brown mascara. "Thank goodness we've still got some time left to enjoy the cease fire!"

"And to spend with our brothers," Amy-Liz said.

"Call them brothers if you want." I smiled. "I, for one, prefer to think of *some* of them as *more* than brothers."

Andie and company turned simultaneously to stare. But I didn't give them a single clue as to what I was thinking.

♥ ♥ ♥

Jared and Todd both hung around during the end-of-camp, late-night hike, walking on either side of me as we made our way up the trail. The rest of my sisters ended up with male counterparts, as well.

I didn't mind sharing the hike with two guys. After all, I'd gone all week without male companionship!

At a rest stop, when Jared was busy talking to Billy, I asked Todd to sit with me on the jeep trip.

"I'd be honored," he said, adjusting his cowboy hat, or was that a gentlemanly tip of the hat?

"And about that duet," I said. "I have a great idea. That is, if you still wanna sing with me."

"We can practice our harmony tomorrow," he said in a slow drawl. I took that as a yes.

"Perfect," I said.

Out of the corner of my eye, I noticed that Jared was looking at us. Apparently, he'd overheard Todd's last words. I didn't dare look at him too closely, but I was sure he was pouting. I could tell from the way his hands were jammed in his pockets. Hard.

I hid a smile. Jared—he never gave up!

❤ · ❤   ❤

Wednesday. Last full day of camp!

The open-jeep ride was even scarier than the brochure advertised. To keep from being too freaked about the steep drop-offs on either side of the trail, Todd and I sang. One song after another.

The jeep stopped at an overlook, and I gasped. "I'm too young to die!"

"I won't let you die, Holly," Todd said, smiling that cowboy grin. "I'm just getting to know you."

It sounded a little hokey, I guess. But that was the part I liked about Todd. Sometimes along with the hokey comes downright honesty.

I thought back to the times when Todd hadn't gone along with the crowd—the guys—and joined in with their jeering. He was his own person. Different from most of the guys I knew, but special just the same. A true gentleman.

We backed up and headed down the same way. I held on to my seat for dear life, convinced my knuckles would stay white forever. Volcanic rock towered above us on switchbacks so narrow that the slightest wrong move by the driver meant a plunge to certain death.

The most comforting aspect of the trip was the way Jared and the rest of our church guys weren't embarrassed about turning ghost-white right along with us girls. No one was being macho about this excursion. The guys were equally freaked! Even Danny, who was heard quoting Psalm 91 for the Miller twins' benefit.

During one of the rest stops, Laina Springer sprang her smile on me. "Heard you figured out who raided your cabin Saturday night," she began.

"Let me guess," I teased.

She blushed. "It was a dumb thing to do," she admitted. "Sorry."

"I think we're all sorry about a lot of things," I said, smiling at her. Billy strolled up just then.

"Well, see ya," I called, feeling good about how

things had turned out with everyone here at camp. And we did survive the jeep trip. Actually, we lived to talk and even laugh about it!

Todd and I ended up singing "Let There Be Peace on Earth" for the talent program—to the accompaniment of his cool guitar. My now-not-so-silent sisters joined in on the ahs and oohs making a fabulous backup for the finale.

The song, the way we arranged it, had never sounded so good. The rest of the guys must've thought so too, because they gave us a standing ovation. It was a far cry from the way they'd treated us before we introduced their sleepy hands to warm H_2O!

I was encouraged. If things kept going this good between all of us, there was hope that the Dressel Hills youth group might actually become super close. Like a family. And what a benefit that would be for all of us.

On the last day of camp, Rhonna and I were alone in the cabin, doing last-minute cleanup. As I swept the wooden floor, I glanced over at her, wondering how she felt about going home. She looked up just then and caught my gaze.

"Rhonna?" I said tentatively. "I just want you to know—I'll be praying for you and your parents."

She smiled. "Thanks. We'll need it."

"I'm no expert at this stuff," I offered. "But things *do* improve over time."

She nodded. "I don't know which hurts worse, watching your parents' marriage crumble at my age, or going through it when *you* did." She looked at me. "You were only eight when your dad left?"

"It seems like another lifetime ago," I whispered, remembering.

"Well, maybe by the time I'm thirty, this'll seem like that for me." She sighed.

"I really hope so, Rhonna, " I said. Then added, "Prayer really helps, you know."

She smiled. "I know."

As for Todd, he walked with me for the last time, carrying my luggage to the bus. I sighed, wishing I'd had more time to get to know him. More time without pacts and wars—for everything.

"Will you write to me?" he asked.

"Sure. I love to write letters."

"I'm not so hot at writing, I guess. But I will, if you write first," he promised.

Wasn't the boy supposed to write first? I thought. "Maybe *you* should write first," I suggested.

"Why?" he said, as we passed the commons area and the dining hall.

"I don't know." I wondered why we were wasting our last precious minutes on silly things like proper procedures for starting a letter-writing relationship.

"I might be able to talk my dad into coming to ski next fall," Todd said, sounding hopeful.

"To Dressel Hills? That'd be fun," I replied. "Maybe the youth group'll be going. You could get to know *all* of us better." I said that only to let him know I wasn't thinking in terms of an exclusive relationship.

Besides, it was time for peace, and that's what I

longed for now. That, and my window seat ... my cat ... and my family. Only not in that order.

Oh ... and a good night's sleep wouldn't feel half bad right about now!

Holly's Super-Duper Snickerdoodle Recipe

makes 3 dozen

For zillions of years these cinnamon-sugar cookies have been known by their silly name. Actually, they started showing up at Dutch tea-tables in colonial times. "They're my favorite cookie in the world," says Holly.

Ingredients:

Mix well—
>1/2 cup soft butter
>3/4 cup sugar
>1 egg

Sift together—
>1 3/8 cups sifted flour
>1 tsp. cream of tartar
>1/2 tsp. baking soda
>1/4 tsp. salt

Set aside—
>2 Tablespoons sugar
>2 tsp. cinnamon

(For high altitudes add 1/4 cup additional flour.)

1. Chill dough one hour in refrigerator.
2. Roll dough into balls the size of small walnuts.
3. Coat balls in sugar and cinnamon mixture.
4. Place about 3" apart on ungreased cookie sheets.
5. Bake at 400 degrees F. till center is almost set and cookie appears lightly browned, 6 to 8 minutes.
6. Cookies will puff up at first, then flatten out with crinkled top.

Hmm, fab-u-lous!

Andie's Mexican Wedding Cookies
(Polvorones)

A festive basket filled with polvorones makes a perfect homemade gift for friends and relatives. Andie dares you to eat just one!

Ingredients:

2 cups all-purpose flour, sifted
1/2 cup confectioners' sugar
1 cup finely chopped pecans
1 tsp. vanilla extract
1/2 cup butter or margarine (room temperature)
1 tablespoon ice water, more or less as needed
confectioners' sugar for garnish

You will need:

1 large mixing bowl
1 mixing spoon
1 nonstick or plain cookie sheet

1. Preheat oven to 350 degrees F.
2. Mix flour, confectioners' sugar, and nuts in large mixing bowl.
3. Add vanilla and butter, using mixing spoon; blend till mixture forms a soft ball. Add tablespoon of ice water if mixture is too crumbly.
4. Pinch off ping-pong-size pieces of dough. Roll into balls in palms of your hands.
5. Place side-by-side on cookie sheet, allowing about 1" between each ball. Bake for about 12 minutes, until set and golden.
6. Remove from oven and sprinkle with lots of confectioners' sugar. Cool before eating.

Enjoy!

❤ What's Your Fashion Signature? ❤

Holly's personal fashion statement is her hair. The waist-length kind. Usually worn in a high ponytail.

Andie's signature is her short, curly do. Kayla globs on the eye makeup. (Look out lashes!) Amy-Liz does something unique—and oh-so-personal—with her feet. Wild, neon-colored socks.

The key to creating your own personal statement with fashion, whether it's a favorite hat, necktie, perfume, or even outrageous socks, is to do it *always*. It'll set you apart from the crowd—give you a fashion fingerprint.

So, dream up something special. But something very *you*. Might be a little crazy. Like earrings on your socks. Yep, earrings make perfect pins—on sweaters, shirts, or scarves. Try 'em on cuffs and collars, too.

Wear hats with safety pins and tiny bows, or bright ribbons and pop beads. Or start a fad and wear mismatched tennies. Or mix and match clashing colors. Why not?

Of course, a personal statement doesn't have to be unusual to be cool. You could wear textured hose, or long skirts and jumpers as your trademark. Or choose a favorite color and go with it for most of your accessories. You might even wanna dress up everywhere you go, like Danny Myers!

Anything goes, as long as it's you!

❤ Holly's Pen Pal Club ❤

Hi! It's me, Holly Meredith, a pen pal freak just like you, and I have a fab-u-lous idea. I've started a pen pal club! Why? Because zillions of girls like you have asked to be linked up with other Christian pen pals who love reading about the stuff that happens to me and my friends here in Dressel Hills.

Now here's the deal. For only four dollars you get two pen pal names and your name will be given to at least one other girl ... plus you'll receive your very own copy of the "Holly's Heart Pen Pal Tip Sheet." This tip sheet is packed with cool ideas for conducting a perfectly successful pen pal friendship.

You probably remember the nightmare I created for myself when I started writing to Lucas Leigh, this older guy in college. For that reason I won't match you up with a guy pen friend. So don't worry—there's absolutely no chance of that!

Grab a pen and follow these instructions:

1. Fill out all the info below.
2. Get your parent's signature (it's required).
3. Cut on the dotted line.
4. Include a self-addressed, stamped business-sized envelope.
5. Send with a four dollar check or money order to:

> Holly's Heart Pen Pal Club
> Attn: Beverly Lewis
> Author Relations
> Zondervan Publishing House
> Grand Rapids, MI 49530

Happy writing!

PLEASE PRINT CLEARLY

Name _____

Street Address _____

City _____ State _____ Zip Code _____

Birthdate _____

Two Hobbies _____

Parent's Signature _____

Don't Miss the Other Holly's

HOLLY'S FIRST LOVE
Book #1 0-310-38051-0
The new boy at school threatens to destroy Holly's relationship with her best friend, Andie. Holly has a secret plan, but when it backfires, she learns the meaning of friendship and the miracle of forgiveness.

SECRET SUMMER DREAMS
Book #2 0-310-38061-8
Holly wants to visit her father in California for the summer, but the idea doesn't make either her best friend, Andie, or her mother very happy. Holly gets some advice from Danny, who seems to have more than just a big brotherly concern. Will Holly make it to California?

SEALED WITH A KISS
Book #3 0-310-38071-5
When Holly and Andie have a pen-pal contest, Holly gets a male pen pal who is in college. To impress him, she lies about her age. He then writes that he is coming to Dressel Hills for a visit. What should Holly do?

THE TROUBLE WITH WEDDINGS
Book #4 0-310-38081-2
Holly's mother is getting married, and Holly is determined to make it a memorable wedding—against her mother's wishes. Meanwhile, Holly tests her former "first love" to see if he's really changed.

CALIFORNIA CHRISTMAS
Book #5 0-310-43321-5
Holly and her sister receive a surprise Christmas invitation to visit their father in California. While there, Holly meets a California surfer, Sean, and her faithfulness to her boyfriend back home is tested.

Heart Books in the Series!

SECOND-BEST FRIEND
Book #6 0-310-43331-2
When Holly's best friend, Andie, invites her Austrian pen pal to Dressel Hills, jealousy erupts as Christiana moves in on Holly's friendship with Andie.

GOOD-BYE, DRESSEL HILLS
Book #7 0-310-44410-1
Holly is moving away from Dressel Hills, and she has just two weeks to say good-bye to all her friends. She wonders whether to continue a "long-distance" relationship with Jared, or to break it off now. To top it off, the surfer she met in California wants to come visit. What should Holly do?

STRAIGHT-A TEACHER
Book #8 0-310-46111-1
Holly develops a crush on the new teacher at school, and he soon becomes the focus of her attention. Her best friend, Andie, wonders if Holly's lead in the spring musical is a result of the handsome teacher playing favorites.

THE "NO-GUYS" PACT
Book #9 0-310-20193-4
It's the summer after eighth grade. Holly's youth group goes to church camp, where Holly and her friends make a pact to ignore the boys for a week. Find out what happens when a hilarious battle of the sexes results! Includes recipes, a pen-pal club, and tips from Holly.

LITTLE WHITE LIES
Book #10 0-310-20194-2
Holly and Andie are in California visiting Holly's dad when Andie falls for an eighteen-year-old surfer. Holly must choose between covering for her friend and telling the truth. Includes an honesty quiz, a pen-pal club, and tips from Holly.